After reading hundreds and hundreds of books on sci-fi, fantasy, historical novels, and reference books, Alan W. Lathan has discovered that the best book to read is the one you write yourself.

This book is dedicated to Marion Zimmer Bradley, who also saw the magic of the ride to Avalon and for all the historical fantasy and science fiction books she wrote and to Jim Butcher for his books on the mad wizard of Chicago.

Alan W. Lathan

Angelina Janny Jones and the Ride to Avalon

Austin Macauley Publishers
LONDON · CAMBRIDGE · NEW YORK · SHARJAH

A CIP catalogue record for this title is available from the British Library.

ISBN 9781398481558 (Paperback)
ISBN 9781398481565 (Hardback)
ISBN 9781398481572 (ePub-e-book)

www.austinmacauley.com

First Published 2024
Austin Macauley Publishers Ltd®
1 Canada Square
Canary Wharf
London
E14 5AA

To all the boys and girls who have read my first book, I do thank you all.

Chapter 1

Day 6 – Allabury Hill Fort

I awoke to the smell of frying eggs and bacon and feeling hunger for the first time in days; I rolled out of the bed only to find I also needed the loo also for the first time since I left Tam Lin days ago. I grabbed my towel and ran into the back of the yurt only to find a hole in the ground and a small stool with a hole in the middle and two buckets. There was a long sponge in water and one bucket was full of woodchips. *Oh my God, how primitive can you be?* There was nowhere else to go so I went on.

So back into the bed and I found a tray of food and drink, *good oh*, and I set to and devoured the lot in no time and as I was finishing the meal Merlin came in. "*Ah, good, you are awake at last. You slept through all yesterday afternoon and most of today. Goewin, my girl, covered you at least once or twice but you must have needed that much sleep with all that essence in you and all the troublesome days you have had to go through, so I hand it to you.*"

As I looked at him, he pulled out of a bag a large dark blue cloak and some long-looking boots and a horse's bridle all in green and gold work. "*Ah, I see you look at my magical horse's bridle. Yes, it is very beautiful is it not? It will calm any mad or nervous horse down to do your bidding and to be one with you. You can ride I trust?"*

"Yes, of course, I can ride a horse, am I not a girl? I have been riding horses since I was eight years old," I told him.

"Oh good, then you will need the fur-lined high-riding boots and the cloak to stop you from getting covered in mud."

"Hey, I do not wear fur, I like all animals."

"Ah, girl, if your ancestors did not hunt, kill, slaughter and cook, eat and wear the hide to survive you would not be here now to say 'I do not like fur'."

"Oh, all right if you insist but only under protest." Just then the girl who I had seen in the hall came to me with a bucket of hot water and towels, still dressed in white, with a comb and straight-edged iron cutting tool and mirror, hair pins and stool. *"Ah, good, Goewin will do up your hair so sit down please."*

So I sat down and asked him, "Can you do something about my hair? Tam Lin's essence turned it to fair and it was all dark brown before."

"Do not worry, it will grow back in time, girl, but not at the moment, as it is good as flaxen pale, just the thing for it is glowing fine after being washed." I had my hair all done up in pins in gold and the headdress as well, which the Merlin said I had to wear if I had to go home. As the girl finished, I thanked her for being kind and doing my hair. As she smiled at me, she opened her mouth and I saw she had no tongue at all. Her eyes wavered in understanding but she never spoke and turned away and left.

"Oh, my poor girl!" I still had the mirror, Roman in origin and original. As I was looking at my hair the Merlin came back with my uniform now all dry and new looking.

"Put this on and do not take it off, please. If you lost any of it and it was found in the future, some archaeologist bod would go nuts. Your school shoes took some cleaning. New leather does not like old magic. The rubber took some convincing to mould back into place, so hurry and get dressed. My boy Brys will escort you down to the horse pens." As he left, I put on the uniform on top of my nightgown and I was all nice and warm. I tried on the fur leggings, they were a bit big on the foot so I put on my shoes first and it was a perfect fit. Next came the cloak with a hood, all fur lined and with a big brooch of silver. Then the Merlin saw me. *"Oh, look at you,"* he said, *"you look very good in the cloak and headdress. I will be glad to see you in the big hall tonight."*

"Why tonight?" I asked.

"There will be a feast in your honour."

"Oh, good God, for me?"

"Yes, now go and see if you can find a horse to your liking, so off you go, " he shouted, *"Boy!"* And his boy came running in. *"Brys, take this Angel to the horse pens."*

"It is Angelina," I said picking up the bridle and began to follow the boy out of the yurt and into a mud hell.

"Oh my, look at the mud." It was everywhere and so I had to pick a way through the worst of it. As I did so, men and women would stop and look and bow to me as I went past. All I could do was nod back. As I looked about me, I saw five of what looked like Iron Age roundhouses and the hall and the smell of burning wood was in the air everywhere as well. Then we came to what they call a palisade, which is a long fence of tall stakes for defence. It had a gate and two guards in late Roman armour with spears and shields who bowed to me. I just nodded to them and stepped out into a stark

11

landscape, all snow and ice. A big hill was on the left side and a wooded deep valley on the right with a brook running up the valley to the hills beyond.

In the lee of the hill was some sort of pen with a group of horses and a ramshackle, *the only way I can describe it*, barn by the looks of it and a mud-ice road running down the side into the valley. There was a horse-breaking ring and some dry stone walls on the sunny side of the hill opposite to a settlement. So, grateful for the riding books, I did not slip up at all till we reached the pen and I stood on some frozen horse dung and, slipping and sliding, I was grasped by a man in a blue cloak and a big wide hat and staff who apparently appeared out of nowhere and held me steady until I found my feet. He then said, "*Careful, lass, you do not want to break a leg at this time.*"

By now I had got familiar with someone or something who just happened to appear out of nowhere and I asked him, "Who are you, please?"

He fixed me with one blue eye. "*I will only say some words to you. The Gods of Asgard are grateful to the mortal lass who with some help will stop the Norn from harming the mortal realms to the extent that they give you a gift of a horse to see you home.*" And he pointed with his staff at a horse at the side of the pen.

Oh, my word! It was a beautiful horse. She was all black with a white nose, of good stock, strong in the legs and heavily built but no more than 13 hands high. As I stood agog at the sight, he whistled and she ran up to us and put her nose into my chest and pushed my cloak to one side, revealing my scarlet blazer. I quickly pulled out the bridle from my blazer pocket and slipped the bridle over her head. "*Who gave you* the halter of *Clynd Eiddyn*?" he asked me, revealing his face for the first time and I saw he only had one eye and a patch over his right one and now I know who this man was.

"The Merlin gave it to me."

"*Ah, I see. Yes, it would seem good sense to give you one of the thirteen treasures of Britain as it will be called by the Merlin. They are said to be kept on his glass house on Bardsey Island.*"

"Please, how do you know so much about me and the Merlin?"

"*I know all that happens in the nine realms, lass, and I know Tam Lin's essence went into the Merlin from you and made him the most powerful wizard of this time.*"

"Please, can you tell me what happened to Tam Lin, please?"

"*Ah, you sent him off to Carterhaugh Wood by the Well of Roses and he was rescued by his true love, Janet from his bondage to the Queen of Fay, which reminds me to have a word with Queen Mab about you as you have had food and wine of Fay which Tam Lin gave you and bound him to you.*"

"Thank you for your kindness this day, All Father, and for the horse and for the wisdom this day," I said as I bowed to him.

"*Ho, ho, I see I cannot pull the wool over your eyes as one as gifted as you mortal but beware the men, women and monsters of this realm, lass, and the Merlin as he will use you for his own ends. They may be called Christians but they are all barbarians and very barbaric at times so be very careful who you speak to and, speaking of talking to anyone, here is something to help you speak YOUR mother tongue. Please, lass, swallow this rune of wisdom with which you will be able to understand all who you speak to.*"

"Please, what is the name of the horse?"

"*Oh, my Valkyries call her Billy Thunder Hoof after her sire. Now swallow the rune.*" So I did and instantly understood all that was being said around me. "*Now I must be off.*" And he whistled and two big wolves ran to his feet and a raven landed on his shoulder. Then he whacked me with his staff. "*Blessings of Odin on you, mortal lass.*" Then he wandered off whistling down the hill.

"*What an interesting old man that was,*" said a voice behind me. As I looked to see who spoke to me, I beheld an even older man who reeked of horse piss and dung and I held my nose. Then he bowed to me and said, "*Does the Lady of the Blue Lake need my service this day?*"

"Oh yes, please. I do need tack and harness, halter and saddle bags and blanket, please."

"*Good. Please do follow me.*" So walking behind him, I lead Thunder Hoof up to the barn and noticed he had a badly pronounced limp. As we walked into the barn, the smell of the harness, saddles, tack and oil made me very homesick and tears welled up in my eyes, so shaking my head, I began to look at what I would need for my journey to Avalon.

I picked out a big blanket, tack, saddle bags and harness then looked at all the saddles. "*This one will do,*" said the man holding up a weird-looking saddle.

"What in God's name is that?" I asked. It was made out of leather and wood with four large horns at the four corners but no stirrups.

"Where are the stirrups?" I asked.

"*Stirrups?*" he said.

"*These are Roman saddles, lady, and no stirrups at all.*"

"But I must have stirrups. I cannot ride without them." He just looked at me.

"*No stirrups, lady.*"

"Oh, never mind," I said. So I threw on what I could onto Thunder Hoof and leading her out, I made my way back up to the yurt. As I walked up to the gate, I remembered to walk to one side of the horse so as not to be kicked by the horse's hooves.

Just then, I heard the boy Brys come running up the road with two buckets of water. He was barefoot but showing no discomfort from the snow and ice as he ran up to me and into the gate. Then I got to the gate and the two guards looked at me and Thunder Hoof, then looked at one another and put down all their weapons and they bowed to me and began to look all over my horse. Then they began discussing the finer points of good horse breeding and good racers or jumpers. Thunder Hoof just stood still as she had probably heard it all before. She draws a lot of people to look at her.

"Good people, please let me pass. I need to see the Merlin." They looked at me in shock then they moved aside to let me pass. So on I walk through the mud up to the yurt.

As I got to the flap the Merlin opened the flap. "*Ah, there you are. What took you so long? Good Gods where did you get an Icelandic pony from?*"

Chapter 2

Day 6 – The Blue Lake

"What? Oh, my pony, mmmm. The Gods of Asgard sent me her as a gift and I was blessed by the All Father for stopping the Norn."

"*By the Gods, you have friends in high places! What? I just made a funny.*"

"Yes, you have. Can I come in please as I am a bit cold?"

"*Yes, yes, come in and the pony as well.*"

So, pulling Thunder Hoof in, I see all the boxes, chests and china cabinets had all been moved to the side of the yurt. "You have been busy," I said as I tied up Thunder Hoof to a post. "Do you have a saddle with stirrups, please?"

"*Oh, you are in luck, come over here, girl.*" So, I followed him over to a big chest I had not seen before which he opened up and inside were weapons, shields, swords, axes, a mail shirt, bow and arrows, helmets and a big red embroidered padded saddle with big cup stirrups.

"Wow, that's a very, very nice saddle," I said.

"*Yes, it was made to fit, tough small ponies. It was designed for horseback archers. As you can see, the saddle is sloped up at the back and forward for shooting arrows accurately using the stirrups.*"

"It is all very good but I do not intend to do any shooting or fighting at all," I said.

He looked at me. "*Girl, you may have to do so. I give you this.*" He pulled out a long curved sword. "*Please have this sword,*" he said.

"No, thank you. But I have a long knife of the Otter God which grew a good six inches or more when I put it next to stupid Excalibur but I left it at the bottom of the lake with my holiday bag."

"*You did what? You left a God-forged dagger at the bottom of the Blue Lake and your bag. Ah well.*" He sat down shaking his head.

"Well, yes. I had no choice at the time."

"*Right, you get that saddle on now we have to go to the lake right away.*" And with that, he stood up, grabbed the saddle and thrust the saddle into my arms.

Quickly, I put it on the pony and went outside the yurt. The flap of the yurt opened and out walked the Merlin in a big black robe with a black staff with two silver dragon heads on it. "Can you help me up, please? I have not ridden wearing a skirt before." And with that, he picked me up and sat me on the saddle then he put my feet into the stirrups.

"*Come on, the day is almost over.*" Now I have not been on a horse for some time what with schoolwork and homework so this was going to be so good. I stood up and tucked my skirt under and sat down, dug in my heels and Thunder Hoof broke into a fast trot and we shot through the gate and into a gallop down the mud-ice road with no difficulty at all. And then there was a boom boom behind me. Ah, now I see why she is named Thunder Hoof.

Suddenly, the Merlin was at my side and shouted, "*I will meet you at the Blue Lake. Keep the hills on your left-hand side, pass the marsh on your right hand and go over the big hill in front of you and you will see the lake.*" And then he was gone and to this day I do not know how he did it. So, urging on Thunder Hoof I let her have her head and with that, she tossed her mane and with flashing eyes, she danced down the road to my delight. It was very cold but great as we shot down the road into a valley. Now I could see the marsh in front of me and turning Thunder Hoof up onto the right, I saw a track running up the hill. We splashed across a stream and she ran up the track past a settlement of some sort. The track now ran up a slope next to a big high hill, then I saw a wall in front of me and Thunder Hoof ran full tilt at it and up and over she jumped. I laughed for the second time only in the last six days.

Then we ran by a very high hill on my left side, then the track ran up a valley onto the big hill in front of me and we galloped up the track to the top and I brought her to a stop. The track ran down a slope and up to a hill so putting Thunder Hoof into a fast trot, we were on to it in no time, we passed a cairn and a stone circle and I saw the Blue Lake below me. In front of me was a very steep descent down into the valley, the track running on my right-hand side was very long and winding leading down into the valley over a ford and following a farm track down to the lake, I rode past a farm and onto the banks and saw the Merlin by the all too familiar jetty.

The lake was all iced up and very blue in colour as I pulled up Thunder Hoof to a stop only to see the Merlin put his head into the Blue Lake. As I dismounted, I told Thunder Hoof to stand as I did so I saw my leggings were all covered in snow, ice and mud. Oh, they do work then as my legs were not at all wet and were still warm.

"*I heard you coming,*" said the Merlin as he stood up. "*I had words with the air spirit and it is willing to let you go in to fetch out the dagger from the bottom, so in you go.*"

"You want me to swim in that cold water? Once was enough," I said.

"*Girl, there is no water in this pool only air as you let free an air spirit into the mortal world. It has absorbed all of the water just to survive.*"

"Oh, I did not know it would be so upset by my letting it out into this realm. Okay, I will go in but only if you melt the ice first, please." So the Merlin melted the ice and then by the edge of the jetty I began to undress. Off with the cloak, then my blazer but my fingers kept sliding off the buttons. "This is silly!" I cried pulling off the leggings.

The Merlin turned around and said, "*You cannot remove any of your clothes, girl, you must not lose any of them at all.*"

"You mean I cannot take off any of my clothes?" I cried. "What about me washing and sleeping?"

"*No, not all. You have to wash yourself and sleep in your uniform till you get to Avalon, girl, so in you go.*"

"Oh God, I hate this world!" I cried as I ran up the jetty and dived into the Blue Lake.

"I just hope no harm will come to my school uniform."

Blue, blue, lots of blue. I could not see anything at all so I surfaced and shouted to him, "I cannot see a thing in this blue air."

"*Ah,*" he said, "*I have this gadget which will help you see most things which cannot be seen normally.*" And he pulled out a pair of what looked like swimming goggles. "*Do not lose these, they are twenty-first-century speaker goggles. Here catch.*" As I caught them I could see a strap at the back so on over my head and, wow, I could see lots better, no more blue at all but clear now all about me.

So back under, I submerged into the now clear air and I can see my bag on the bottom in the weeds so down I swam to it and picked it up. Now for my dagger. I can see it stuck in the mud. So over to it I swam, not too far away. As I reached for it, a horrible face appeared in front of me. A large, waterish round bloated face like a pearl and I knew it was the air spirit itself. "*Now I go,*" said a voice and all the blue disappears leaving clear water and a pearl.

"No, no!" I cried, grasping the dagger and pulling it out of the mud. Instantly, I was in freezing cold water again, then the pearl shot into my gasping mouth and I swallowed the stupid thing.

Here I go again. Up to the surface, dagger point upright into the ice and hacked my way through to the surface and come up gasping for breath and began to break the ice back to the jetty. It was then I heard laughter. I looked up to see the Merlin roaring with laughter and I shouted, "This is not funny!" as I punched the ice up to the jetty.

"Help me out please, now."

"*Oh ho, what a laugh you gave me,*" he said as he pulled me out of the lake. "*Nice looking dagger you have. Come on back to the barn with you,*" he said, wrapping my cold body up in my warm cloak. He picked up my boots and put them on Thunder Hoof's saddle, said something to the pony who set her eyes then he grasped my cold hand and the pony, saddle and me all appeared back in the yurt.

"Oh good God, what was that," I said as I ran to the fire to get warm once more, dripping water and shivering as I pulled off my cloak and sat by the fire.

"*Goewin, Brys, come here now!*" shouted the Merlin as he tied up my pony to a post and they both came running in.

"*Brys, rub down the pony and feed her. Now, Goewin, hot wine now please.*" As she ran out, he went over to the bathtub and turned on the taps and hot water flowed out.

I was sitting by the fire and I could not see any pipes going into the bathtub at all and I asked, "Where does the water come from, please?"

"*What? Oh, from a hot spring in Iceland, girl. Now off with that wet uniform and into the tub, please.*"

"You said I could not take it off."

"*Inside the yurt, you can, but not outside. In you get.*" Just then, the girl ran in with a pot of wine and a red hot poker and two cups. She put them onto a table and put the hot poker into the pot of wine. "*Ah good. Hot wine, this will warm you up.*"

As I began to take off my wet uniform, the girl ran over to me and held up the cloak for me, looking daggers at the Merlin and, wrapped in my cloak. I got in the bath and gave the cloak to Goewin and sank into the suds. *Ah, ah, lot's better.* As I lay in warm happiness, I watched the girl hang my uniform on a pole on the roof over the fire and I thought, *It is going to smell of smoke again!*

Then the Merlin handed me a cup of hot wine to drink. *Wow! Nice fruity taste to it.* Then I asked him what did he say to the Air Elemental because it appeared to me as I was in the blue and it said "*I go now*" and shrunk down to a pearl and shot into my mouth. "*Did it? Oh well, not to worry, girl, it will come out in its own time I imagine. So let's have the headdress off so you can wash your hair.*" And with that, he pulled it off and hung it up with my uniform to dry. Goewin came over to wash me and my hair with a warm towel. She poured into the bath some fragrant sweet-smelling liquid then she rubbed me all over with a sponge until I was shining.

The Merlin came in carrying a long white dress, my armband and a gold brooch with colourful enamel inlays with a big pin and a gold belt and a pair of long-looking sandals with straps which he gave to Goewin. "*Put these on when you are dry as your uniform is too wet for the feast tonight.*" The arm ring I had received from Tam Lin now had five red jewels in place of the pearls and the black ruby and I asked him why I had to wear the arm ring as he had said it was not of this world. "*Ah,*" said he, "*I have placed an illusion on it to appear as a normal-looking ring and you will need it to hold up the standard as it still has the strength of ten men in it, so here, put it on, please.*"

I put out my arm and he pushed it a long way along, over my elbow. "That hurt!" I cried.

"*No pain, no gain,*" he said, "*and the rubies will enable you to enter the shimmering divide between worlds to get into the Isle of Avalon to the other world unseen by mortal men.*"

"Is that the reason I have to dress as a priestess of Avalon, to get to the Holy Well?" I asked him.

"*Yes,*" he said.

"Oh well, I will if you say so."

"*Then out you get and Goewin will do your hair up for you for the feast tonight so hurry up and put on the dress please.*" So out of the bath, hair done up, sandals on, dress down to my knees, a belt of gold around my waist and the now dry headdress on and then my blue cloak as well and all done. Brys and Goewin ran off somewhere so I had a look at Thunder Hoof who had on a feedbag and was munching away on her feed. Her bed of hay was all laid out for her already so I gave her a rub down to pass the time and with my bone comb did her dock and mane. "*Oh, there you are,*" said the Merlin, "*I have found a dagger scabbard big and long enough to fit the dagger of yours.*" And he handed it to me. "*Hang it on your belt,*" he said. Just then Brys and Goewin came in both all dressed in white. "*Right, all ready, are we? So off we go to the feast.*"

To the door, we all trooped and outside to mud city and I stopped. "How am I going to make it to the hall in these sandals?" I asked. And with that, the boy and girl lifted me up by my armpits and carried me across the mud to the door with no difficulty. Then I heard a horn blowing from inside the hall and we opened the leather flap to the door and the Merlin pulled me forward and pushed me into the hall.

Everybody inside looked at me and they all bowed as I entered, then the girl slave gave to me a cup of mead and I said, "Oh, how kind of you," in old English. She looked at me in shock and backed away from me and ran over to a sideboard which was full of food and drink in pots and bowls and loaded with round bread.

"*Come with me,*" the Merlin said and we came to the top table.

There stood the Duke and his Duchess dressed in green who seized hold of my head and said, *"Greetings, Angel. You are heaven-sent. Please say the Lord's blessing to start the feast for us."*

"Oh, Okay," I said and then I stood in front of the table and turned to all the people in the hall and said the Lord's prayer and blessed the feast to lots of shouting and banging on the tables.

Then the feast began with slaves and women serving the top table first. I sat down by the Merlin on his right side, the Duchess on my left and I sipped my honey mead then was given a round bit of bread and I ask the Merlin what it was for. *"For your food,"* he said, *"just put it in the top and all the juices soak in the bread so you can eat it all through the feast."*

"I see," I said drinking my mead down and looking for more. The Duke handed me a drinking horn full of mead which I put to my lips and drank the lot, much to the amazement of the Duke, who then laughed out loudly.

The Merlin turned to me. *"Ease up on the mead or you will be drunk in no time."*

The Duchess turned to me and said, *"Can you sing for the clan, please? Something from your home, some heavenly song would be nice, Angel."*

"Oh, can I please and call me Angelina as well if you please." Then the food or stew appeared on top of my bread placed there by a grinning Brys who was serving the top table. I picked up a spoon with a funny handle.

The Merlin saw me look at it and said, *"That is a Roman swan dip spoon, girl, the neck is lower at the handle making a swan neck."*

"Oh I see," but no forks to be seen. "Are there no forks?" I asked him.

"*They have not been invented yet but you can have this.*" And he put his head into his robe and pulled out a serving fork, "*here, you can keep it.*"

"Oh good," I said looking at it and I read on the back, "made in Sheffield Stainless Steel." And looked at him. "You are funny sometimes." So I dug into the food and ate the lot till I was full and sat back to look around.

I saw a man dressed in a long plaid coat carrying a harp who had just come into the hall. He was looking at me. "Who is that?" I asked the Merlin.

"*It is the bard from Eriu? Oh, I mean Ireland. Um, bard sings a song for the hall.*" So the bard bowed, sat down and performed and played some nice tunes.

Then the lady in green stood up and said, "*Come with me, Angel.*" So I got up and walked to the front of the table with her and she said, "*this is Angel who will sing for you all.*" And there was lots of banging of knives and spoons. So I stood up straight, which took some doing and sang some religious songs, ones I could remember. At the end, I had some more mead and I gave the lot Danny Boy and the Ballard of Young Tam Lin all the way through as I had sung it to Tam Lin only three days ago and I had to finish with Jerusalem. The applause was deafening with clapping and approval.

Then I sat back down in my chair, had some more mead and slipped down under the table to much laughter and I was out, drunk.

Chapter 3

Day 7 – Crosses

I awoke with someone poking me in the ribs. "*Wake up girl, you have been asleep for too long, now get up.*"

As I opened my eyes, pain shot through my head. "Aaagh! My head hurts." And I hung my head down.

"*Here, drink this girl.*" A cup was put into my hands. "*Drink it all up now.*" So I did. *Wow, it was coffee, nice and hot and sweetened with sugar and so nice.*

As my head cleared I saw the Merlin holding a bacon bun and he said, "*You had so much mead to drink at the feast that you fell out of your chair too much merriment, so eat your bun and hurry up and get dressed, girl.*" Drinking the coffee was nice and I ate the bun. Then I noticed I was naked and I heard someone come in so I covered myself up only to see Goewin with my uniform and cloak, boots, headdress, belt and dagger. As she approached, she gestured to me then to herself indicating she had undressed me after the feast. *Good,* I thought. Then she gestured to the stool, put all my clothes on the bed and ran off only to appear with a bowl of hot water for my wash and I had an all-over wash, my hair done up with gold pins again and on with the headdress. Then it was time to put all my clothes back on and I recalled I could not take them off again until I got to Avalon. Oh well, so on I put everything but I left my blazer undone for once to see what would happen.

Once I was fully clothed, I went to find Thunder Hoof only to see her already saddled, harnessed, girth done up, groomed with saddle bags and sleeping roll, food bag and some hay with a grinning Brys standing by her. Thunder Hoof gave me a good greeting and I gave her a hug and a kiss on the nose and I gave Brys one too. Then I noticed a pair of riding gloves and a helmet of some kind on the saddle. The flap of the yurt opened up and in came the Merlin. "*Ah, you are ready I hope. The Troop is ready to go.*"

"Go where?" I replied.

"*To Avalon, my girl, so on your pony now, please.*"

"Where to first?" I ask him.

"*Oh, you have to bless some crosses first.*"

"Pardon, do what to crosses?"

"*Bless them, girl. This part of the world is full of them.*"

"Oh great," I muttered. So, grabbing the halter, I led Thunder Hoof outside only to see a large troop of horsemen in Dark Age armour, shields, helmets, spears, javelins, swords – the lot and I stood in disbelief to see such a breath-taking sight.

Then the Merlin said, "*Come up to the front with you now.*" So pulling Thunder Hoof past the troop I saw the Duke and the Lady in Green holding up a long pole with a red flag with the Star Dragon, Uther Pendragon's sign. The Lady in Green handed the pole to me.

"*Hail the Golden Angel!*" she cried as she turned to the troop who roared their approval.

The Duke then gave me a big hairy hug and when he saw my horse, his eyes went wide. He had a good look at Thunder Hoof and examined the saddle and the stirrups and said, "*This is not made of wood but iron.*" And he turned to the Merlin. He said something about the saddle and stirrups, pointed at the pony and me then he shouted for the blacksmith and a big, bald man ran up and they bowed, inspected the stirrups and saddle and then the blacksmith ran off.

Ah ha, this Mongolian horse's saddle and stirrups have let the cat out of the bag, I thought. "*Oh oh,*" said the Merlin, "*you have made a big insight on horse harness and tackle, my girl, they are still on Roman saddles with no stirrups as well.*"

"Please, what is the helmet for?" I ask.

"*So you do not fall off and break your neck, my girl. It is very old, at least 500 years. It was at the beach when Julius Caesar landed at Kent back in 55BC. On some mad Celt head in his chariot no doubt.*"

"If it is old it cannot be much good now then, can it?" I ask him.

"*Oh, you would be surprised how good it can be.*" And with that, he put it on my head and pulled my hood up over it and handed me the riding gloves. "*You will need these for your hands and by the way, they all liked it when you sang Parry's Jerusalem.*"

"Oh good," I said as I put my foot into the stirrup and swung into the saddle, hooked up my skirt and sat down. Thunder Hoof did a dance, eager to be off. As I put my right foot in the right-hand stirrup, the young slave girl ran up to me.

"*For you, lady,*" she said and handed me a bag full of cakes.

29

"Thank you," I said to her. She smiled at me and ran off. I put the butt of the pole to the ground and looked in to find lots of flat cakes but one big one, nice looking and fat and round and still warm so I took a bite. "Oh good, apple pie." I took a biggish bit and chomped – ouch my teeth. I pulled out of my mouth a long silver chain with a very small hammer attached to it. "Oh oh." I looked around for the girl but she was nowhere to be seen so I put it into my blazer pocket with the bag of cakes, picked up the pole and into a fast trot up to the front of the troops who were all mounted up.

At the front, the Duke was on his big Andalusian horse, sitting on one of those big roman saddles with the four horns and no stirrups and I thought, *how do you ride in one with no stirrups?*

I nodded to him and Thunder Hoof said hello to the Andalusian. "Nice horse," I said.

"*Yes,*" he said. "*He is an Iberian stallion.*" Then he looked at my school blazer badge and I saw his lips move. "*Ah,*" he said, "*trust and justice and goodwill to all men,*" he said in Greek Latin, "*words by Socrates the Athenian Philosopher. Good words you have on you, now let's go.*" And with that, we all move out of Allabury Hill Fort then turned left out the doors and down a stony slope to a farm.

At the farm, we turned left down a muddy lane to a river. The lane led down to a ford not too deep but fast flowing, then up a steep hill to a hamlet of six huts. "*Trebartha,*" said the guide and up to one side were five small crosses.

"*Would you please, my angel, say a few words to the Troop?*" Duke said as they all gathered around me.

"Oh, all right." So I dismounted and did what the Pope did in Rome, and blessed the cross then the Troop who all hung their heads and crossed themselves.

Blessing done, I mounted Thunder Hoof but I forgot to tuck my skirt under then the duke said, "*Away.*" And off we trotted up a lane lined with old bramble all brown with age and as I rose to the trot my skirt rose up with the wind blowing cold up my behind. Not very nice at all, I need to do something about it, oh for a pair of jodhpurs.

As I rose up and down to the trot, the Duke looked at me. "*What are you doing, my angel?*"

31

"Where I come from we rise to the trot, my lord. I can sit if you do not like it." So I sat and did what they do in the USA, the sitting trot to please him.

In time, we came to a bigger hamlet with a church and burial ground on my left side. As we rode in, there were lots of people and horses next to a stone hut and as we approached, they all stood up and bowed to the Duke and me. Everyone but me dismounted so I turned to the Duke. "Please what is happening now?" I asked him.

"*My angel, we all go to the church,*" he said, "*it being Sunday.*" Oh, I had no idea it was a Sunday as I had lost all track of time but yes I said to myself since I fell down into the water tube five or six days ago.

I dismounted off Thunder Hoof and loosened the gift and gave her a pat. Brys ran up to me and took the bridle from me and the pole from me and ran off. "*Oh, there you are,*" said the Merlin. "*Nice ride was it not and welcome to Herte or Bre-Gledlh,*" he said, "*but I call it North Hill, charming village. Come on into the pub and get warm.*" So I followed him into a large room full of men doing what men do best: drink. As we went in, they made room for us to get to a room at the back, where I was pushed onto a stool and given a cup of hot wine to drink. In the room with me was the Duke and a small person who looked like a priest who was sitting down at a table looking at me with a strange look on his face.

"*My angel can sing words from heaven,*" said the Duke as he turned to me. "*Please, my angel, show him your scarlet tunic.*" Oh, okay so off with my hood and cloak and the old helmet, spread my hair out and stood up straight for him to see my scarlet school blazer.

"Oh my God! The Emperor's royal scarlet. How extraordinary," he said as he stood up. *"How is it possible to have an angel in my home?"* And he shook with joy.

"Easy," said the Merlin. *"She is from a different realm than ours. Because she is blessed by your God and the Virgin Mary and by the great virgin goddesses so we are blessed by her presence, who has seen more evil things than you or I will ever see and vanquish more forces with the Sword of Light."* I just looked at him in disbelief.

What is he going on about? Yes, I have seen more than I would like to see in the last week to last a lifetime but he is laying it on a bit much.

"My angel, would you please lead my boys up to the church with Galen's permission and agreement," said the Duke.

"Yes, yes of course," said the priest who jumped up at once. *"Please it would be my pleasure."* So up he got up and ran off very happy.

"Yes, I would," I said to the Duke as I drank my hot wine and made a face at the taste.

"Haha." Laughed the Duke. *"No, love for wine but mead I see, haha."* I just helped myself to some bread and cheese that the Merlin had put on the table. *"Yes, eat up, we have a long ride today,"* said the Duke.

After the church service, where I had to sing some more songs and bless the church and a well, all the men were in the inn drinking as men do. I made my way out to the horse lines. The number of horses were of all different breeds of British native ponies and horses with no horseshoes at all, how odd. I looked at all of them and even Thunder Hoof had no shoes. Sitting down on the saddle, I went through my saddle bags to find my bag. Inside was a white bag with peppermints in and no need now to know who put them in, so I popped one in the horse's mouth and she gave me a look of joy. "Well," I said, "no peppermints in Asgard, you poor pony." Then all the men came out of the inn and began to saddle up so I did the same thing and loaded up Thunder Hoof and got on remembering to tuck my skirt in and under me. Brys ran up and gave me the pole then ran up to the inn, so I turned Thunder Hoof up to the front of the troop as the Duke came out of the inn with the Merlin.

"*My horse,*" called out the Duke and a man ran with his big horse and he grabbed the horns on the saddled and vaulted onto the horse. "*We go,*" he called and off we went up a lane which ran up to a snow-covered hill past a hill farm set down a slope. We turned right at the bottom into a valley covered in snow but still good going. Back up one more slope onto a track. Here some more horsemen came down from a hill fort and all bowed to the Duke. We followed the track for some time until the Duke turned to the right into one more valley and he looked at a cross of about four feet high. I had to do the blessing of the cross and the troop and then back up on my pony. We all followed up the valley to a big-looking hamlet with a church. "*Lewannick,*" said the Duke. As we rode in, I saw a big standing stone by the side of the track all inscribed in Latin but we did not stop to look at it. The church was on a raised oval mound, made all of the wood with a pillar outside. As we rode in, some men ran up to the Duke.

Chapter 4

Day 8 – The Hole then Lunch

"*Help, help!*" they all cried.

"*Please help us. There is a big monster, huge and ugly up on the hill by the sheep pens. Can you help?*"

"*Yes, of course. We will dismount, lads,*" said the Duke to the troop. He turned to me, "*Stay on the pony but keep by my side.*"

"Right oh," I said as we all followed the men who appeared to be shepherds by their woollen clothes as they led us to a large snow-covered sheep pens by a large hill with many rocky outcrops.

As we approached the pens, I could see some brown sheep all huddled by the side of the pen in terror and no wonder because of the blood on the snow and some big footprints in the snow. "*It ate two of my best sheep!*" cried one of the shepherds. "*And hopped off to the hill with two more under his arm. Can you help save them, my lord?*"

"*Swords out!*" cried the Duke as we followed the footprints up to a dark hole in the side of the hill.

"*My angel, go to the back of the line if you would please,*" said the Duke. So I turned Thunder Hoof back around to stand with the shepherds who were warming their hands and looking very cold. Me, I was nice and warm and sat on top of Thunder Hoof. One thing I will say about horses, they are very nice and warm.

The Duke and his men began to look into the dark hole then out of the darkness flew a dark shape straight out of the hole and ran under the Duke's legs, making him fall over. Then a big roar came from inside the hole and hopping out of the hole came the most harrowing-looking thing. Its appearance was very striking. It had one big leg placed centrally under its body and one arm sprouting from the middle of its chest, one eye was in the middle of its face and a single tuft of tough hair rose from the top of its head. In its hand was a big wooden cup.

"Bloody hell, what is it?" I cried as I saw the sheep which had run into the Duke run over to the sheep pen and jump in to join his fellow sheep. One of the Duke's men began to pull him up but the big monster thing did a sweeping blow with its cup, hitting the man to the ground. As all the rest of the men charged in with their swords, spears, axes and arrows, Thunder Hoof started to quiver and tremble under me in excitement as she saw the fighting and I pulled out my dagger in readiness and it was glowing red.

As I watched the fighting, I could see it was going perilously badly for the men as all their weapons were doing no harm to the monster at all and I saw its big foot holding down the Duke so he could not use his sword at all and it was sweeping its cup to keep the men off. I knew what to do and turning Thunder Hoof to the left, I trotted her over to the far side of the fight and turned her to face the monster, pushed the pole into the snow and put my dagger into my right hand and said, "Go," to Thunder Hoof who broke into a fast trot and we were soon pounding down and into the gallop with Thunder Hoof booming beneath me as we charged into the skirmish. *Wha-hay.*

And would you believe it? All the men stopped fighting to look at me as we thundered down to the monster who looked up to see us and I stood up in the stirrups to cut under its kneecap and with a perfect penetration cut the hamstring. The monster bellowed in rage and fell over onto its back. The Duke leapt up out of the snow and with one blow of his sword beheaded the monster to the cries of his men. I reined in Thunder Hoof, who started to dance to the trot up and down in the snow, loving the moment.

"*All hail the Golden Angel!*" cried the Duke as he and his men all ran up to me.

I was plucked out of the saddle and held up on the men's shoulders who all cried, "*Hail the Blue Angel!*" And Thunder Hoof did a horse laugh to see such fun. The shepherds then joined in the joyful moment until the monster's body all but dissipated into thin air with lots of spectacular lights and the hole rolled back up until nothing but the snow was left to be seen.

Then I was dumped to the ground and all the men looked at the spectacular sight, as one they all crossed themselves and made the sign of the horns. Me, I got back onto my pony and trotted over to the pole, pulled it out and trotted over to the Duke and said, "That made me very ravenous, when's lunch?"

"*Haha!*" they all cried.

"*The shepherds can feed us all,*" said the Duke looking at the shepherds who all nodded their assent so with that we all trooped off to the brightness of the huts in the hamlet. After seeing to the horses' needs in some nearby horse pens and hobbling them, I gave Thunder Hoof a peppermint for being a good horse.

In one of the huts, we were given some hot food by the women of the hamlet. We had stew in wooden bowls, mainly lamb stew but with no potatoes at all and I asked, "Where are the potatoes?"

"*What are potatoes?*" someone said. On, no, I realised potatoes came from South America and tomatoes as well and would not be in use until 1600 AD and I did a quick sum in my head. *Oh my God, no potatoes until 1200 years' time. Oh my!*

After lunch, we all went into the church, which was on a mound and made out of wattle and daub or manure and wood bark mixed in water and splatted on by hand as I have done it at school camp. Then we did a quick service and a visit to Blaunder's well where we watered the horses and filled up all the drinking flasks and skins, and back on the horses me and the troop set off on our way. When we came to a cross on the way on the top of a hill, I had to do a blessing once more.

We went down a hill to a ford and splashed over and up a slippery slope. "Oh look, another pigging cross!" I was getting pee'd off with all these crosses. As the Merlin said, Cornwall is full of them. So I had to do the same thing again, bless the darn thing and sing to the troop once more. Back on, we rode all afternoon passing four hamlets on the way but we did not stop at all. By now, I was getting a bit saddle-sore. As the day came to an end, we hit upon a hamlet with a church where I saw some large tents set up for the night. Good, at last, I can rest.

Chapter 5

Day 7 – The Visitation

As I had not ridden for some time, I was bow-legged and sore in lots of places as I dismounted Thunder Hoof. She looked as fresh as a daisy. I undid the girth and pulled off the saddle, placed it on the ground and led her to the horse pens for the night. As I went to pick up my saddle, I saw all the men putting their saddles around a campfire so I did the same and then sat down with the pole still in my hand so I rammed it into the ground and looked into my saddle bags for something to eat and drink.

Sometime later, one of the men asked me to sing something to them so I gave them all the songs I could remember and we all sat around the fire and sang. Then the Duke came to me. *"You need your sleep, my angel, we have a big ride tomorrow. Go to your bed now, please."* So he led me to a tent for the night, I rolled out my bedroll and was soon asleep.

I woke up. "Aghh!" I cried. "I need to pee." I rolled out of bed, put my cloak on and staggered out of the tent to see the moon was up and so I could see the woods where the loos were. Then I ran into one of the guards.

"Whoa, Angel, where are you going?"

*"*The loo," I said, "where is it please?"

"*Come on.*" So with his torch, he led the way over to the edge of the dark wood.

"Okay," I said, "I can manage by myself from here on."

"*Do not go too far. There is a slope down to the river not far in,*" he said.

"All right, I will not go too far in." So into the wood, I felt my way to the trees to do my loo by a big tree. I was pulling myself up when a little blue round globular glowing light approached me and did a dance in front of my eyes. I was compelled to follow the light into the woods down a slippery snow-covered slope, down to a river, and splashed my way over to an upward slope going on my hands and knees and climbing up to the top of the wood still following the light.

Then it stopped by a big dolman, three upright stones and a big capstone on top. It was an old tomb on top of the hill. Then the light shot into the tomb and I awoke to find myself on top of a hill with no snow at all. Then there was a big clap of thunder over my head and rain plummeted down onto me. "S**t!" I cried pulling my hood over my head and ran for shelter in the tomb. I ran in and out of the rain until my nose hit something soft, very wet and very big. Jumping back, I pulled my hood back down and looked up to see a very big horse. As the blue light lit up the tomb, I saw two more big horses on either side and on top were two large men in what looked like armour with long spears.

But sitting on the horse in front of me in all her glory was Queen Mab of the Fay, Queen of the Seelie court, and Shakespeare's Titania Fairy Queen of the Midsummer Night's Dream. *Oh my!* "I give greetings to the Queen of the Fay, well met by moonlight," I quoted.

"Greetings, mortal child. We meet at last." And her voice was as cold as a mountain stream in winter. *"Welcome to my world, mortal child. I thank you for the return of young Tam Lin following his release from incarceration by the Norn in the Tree of Life. I see by my sorceries you have been busy. Not only have you defeated one Otter God, the Norn and the troll and my Fachan who ate only three sheep and with some help from someone who I will not name here in my realm. You have on you something which is owed to me, which was given into Tam Lin's keeping to defeat the Norn."* At this point, I remembered my manners and I bowed very low.

"Greetings to the Queen of the Fays," I said as I stood up and then I saw I was no longer on top of the hill in winter but on a sunlit summer's day on a hill in the realm of the Fay.

"Mortal, I now release you from Tam Lin's pledge of your maidenhood to him." And with that, she hit me with a witch hazel wand, *ouch.* *"But know this, mortal, she who is out of time should make time to stop it. Now, I know the sword of the Fay is lost to us for some time but it will come back to us in time to do its work. Now hold out your arm, child, so I can take my arm ring off you and the air spirit as well and why are you dressed as a priestess of Inys Witrin, the Isle of Glass, your Glastonbury?"*

"I am sorry but I cannot remove my blazer to remove it. The Merlin has put a spell on my school uniform until I get to Avalon or Glastonbury, I hope all the way by horse so I can take it off."

"What the one who is the Merlin?" And with that, she was off her horse and loomed over me as I leaned back she seized my right arm and pushed back my sleeve of the blazer to see

the arm ring and hissed in anger and jerked her hand back in some haste.

"*Aahh, wizard magic!*" she cried.

"*Rubies set in cold iron, the Merlin knew I would call you to me at some time. Aahh, now I know why he has sent you on your way to Inys Witrin, so he can get back into the sanctuary. But why you, child? What is so special about you? Hold out your left hand, child.*" So I did and she looked at the palm of my hand. "*That explains it.*"

"What do you mean, it explains it?" I asked her.

"*You are of the lineage of Bendigeid Farn or Bran the Blessed, whose head is buried at the White Tower at Londinium. Child, you are of ancient lineage, which is why you are so special and are able to do all the things you have done so far. You are a daughter of the sea god Llyr.*"

"But what do you mean by ancient lineage? My dad comes from Newport."

"*Maybe so, child, but you can do extraordinary things by your lineage, something even I cannot do with all my power over time and space. But you child, you can be very useful to the Fay for she who has partook of food and drink of the Fay are not so easily cast aside for inside of you is my Air Spirit, which must be returned to its ownership of the Great Pandasha at the Palace of Ten Thousand Pearls, who I acquired it from so you must return it to her so she can remove it from you safely.*"

"Oh please, can you tell me how to as I swallowed it down as it appeared to me in the lake and said, 'Now I go.' What did it mean and who is this Great Pandasha?"

"*Ah well, you mortal will have to go to her yourself. I will give you the means for you to transport to her realm but first,*"

43

we must let the Merlin perform his little play at Inys Witrin. Now then, I have something that you would call Fairie dust. Only use it for calling me at times when you need it most." And with that, she pulled out a bag from inside her robes. *"Keep it safe from sunlight child and only cast it onto the water for me to see you."*

"Yes, I can put it into my school blazer inside pocket," I replied. So I pulled back my cloak to reach inside to unzip my pocket and took out a plastic bag. Inside was a spare button, a sewing kit with needles and thread which my mother must have put in for me, which will be very useful in time, so I put the bag inside sealed it up and put it back in my inner pocket and zipped it up.

"I see now why the Duke has taken a shine to you with that purple blazer and blue plaid skirt. No wonder he calls you his angel. He thinks you come from Heaven to help him win his war."

"War, what war?" I ask her.

"Tomorrow in your world you will be at the site of Slaughter Bridge. He will confront his brother Uther Pendragon to help him to regain his throne from King Vortigern, who is in what you call Wales. It is a stupid name as it means stranger in Anglo-Saxon."

"No, it is not a stupid name at all. We in Wales are proud of our heritage so there!" I shouted at her, forgetting who I was shouting at.

"Oh my, oh my, what an independent little hussy you are. Good, I like it. You are not afraid to speak your mind to one as I, yes, yes, you will be very useful to the Fay, the All Father said you were not alarmed by powerful malevolent beings."

"Ah," I said, "that is because in the last eight days I have seen seven or more beings and monsters enough to last me a lifetime and I am still standing." Her laughter was loud and horrible to hear as I pushed my fingers into my ears.

"*You make me laugh, mortal child. I have not laughed so much in many a year. So now I mark you as my vessel to do my bidding.*" And with that, she hit me again with her wand on top of my head. I felt the same force of power flowing to me as Tam Lin's did to me but not too bad this time as I did not fall asleep or fall over, only shuddered all over. "*Child, keep your maidenhood pure and flawless please, without it you will be powerless to act for me.*" Then I was compelled to go down to my knees to acknowledge her gift to me. "*Also, I give you one of my rings of ancient acknowledgement to see you safely to Inys Witrin so go now, child, I will see you again.*"

Then I found myself kneeling down in wet snow as I looked up, the tomb had gone, so jumping up I find myself bloody freezing cold in a foot of snow. Looking around, I saw my footprints coming up the hill and wrapping my cloak around me I began to follow them down some woods into a deep valley bottom. All was dark but I was aware of flickering lights in the distance on top of the hill in the woods.

Down to a river, I had to splash my way over as my shoes and socks were all wet from the snow, I did not worry too much, then up the slope into the woods. Then I heard my name being called. "Here!" I shouted and a man ran down to me with a fire torch.

"*Over here!*" he cried as he made his way to me he stopped and looked at me and made the sign of the cross and backed away. Then all the Duke's men appeared and I was helped up through the woods, up to the camp and put by the fire to warm up.

Then the Duke approached me. *"My angel, what happened to you? My men were looking for you for hours when you did not come out of the woods."*

"Ah well," I said, "would you believe it, I have had a visitation by Queen Mab, the Queen of the Fay this night so I may be a bit stricken by her power." With that, I opened my cloak for all to see me glowing in the dark with Mab's essence on me. The effect was not what I expected as they all crossed themselves and fell into kneeling all around me. Very embarrassing.

"Please, please, all stand up!" I cried.

"All I have is some essence, her ring of power to see me to what did she call it, Inys Witrin." At that, they all stood up. "Well, good night to you all." And I made my way to my bed and fell at once into a deep sleep.

Chapter 6

Day 8 – The Bridge

Food sizzling in the pan was the first thing I heard as I lay in my bed in the morning and as I rolled out I found myself as hungry as a hunter.

I quickly got on my riding boots and gloves, picked up my saddle and crazy helmet and ventured out into the early morning sun, chilly but fresh, and over to the cooking fires. I was greeted by lots of, "*Good morning, Angel. We trust you slept well. We did not after last night.*" I was given some food on a roll of bread to eat, a bit hard but I ate out of necessity. It was mutton, I hope, inside the roll. After eating, I went to find Thunder Hoof who gave me a good welcome. As I kissed her on the nose, I let her kiss me back then I gave her a good grooming all the way over and her forelock, carefully cleaned out her hooves then I gave her the nosebag to eat her feed.

When all was ready, the Troop moved off, me and the Duke up in front rose up onto a flat moorland where there was a strong wind blowing up my cloak and skirt. *I must do something about that in time.* This was only a short ride to a place called Clether with a holy well and two crosses, which I had to bless and sing some more. All through the morning, I saw the Duke looking at me with a strange look. From then on, we rode up a river valley to one more cross and what the Duke called an ancient stone enclosure, one more building and over a river where good old Thunder Hoof began to splash river water all over me to the laughter of the Troop. "Stop it you mad horse!" I cried as she began to toss her head and dance over the bank up a long slope and with that, we began to trot for a bit, then into a canter at an easy pace for four miles or more and stopped by a river to water the horses.

"*My angel,*" said the Duke. "*Do be careful from now on, please. Do cover up the Emperor's purple. I do not want my brother to see you in all your splendour as yet.*"

"Very well, I will do as you ask, but why may I ask you?"

"*Because, my angel, I am in disgrace for losing my kingdom to King Vortigern the usurping King of Britain who united the Saxons as mercenaries to fight against the invading Picts and Scots.*"

"So what happened then?" I asked him.

"*Oh, the Saxons soon became greedy for land and began inviting more of their kind to join them.*"

"And what did King Vortigern do?"

"*He fled his kingdom when the Saxons rose up in rebellion and he attempted to arrange a peaceful meeting between the Britons and the Saxons at the Giants Dance in the middle of my kingdom but the Saxons bought hidden weapons into the council and at a signal rose up and massacred the unarmed Britons.*"

"Mmm, Sorry. You said a Giants Dance. Where is it?" I asked.

"*It is a big ancient stone circle of menhirs, massive stones set up on end as a monument to the sun and the moon.*"

"Oh, you mean Stonehenge in Wiltshire? I went there on a school trip last year as the school camp was on Salisbury Plain."

"*I do not know the name of this place you speak of but henge or Stonehenge is a good name for the Giants Dance. Now put your hood over your head and do follow me.*"

So on we rode up a muddy lane for a bit. Then the Duke said, "*Please do dismount.*" And all the Troop did likewise and hobbled all the horses. I got off and put the stirrups up and loosening the girth, I led Thunder Hoof over to the horse lines being set up. "*Please do come with me,*" said the Duke, "*and bring my standard with you.*" So on we walked down the muddy lane, around a corner, the lane ran down to a deep river valley very sharply here. At the bottom was an old bridge where the lane ran over and up a sharp slope, up to an enclosure which was teeming with men in cloaks and horses with a standard just like the one I was holding. "*Do come on, I want to get this over with.*" So down the lane, we all tramped to the bridge. As we approached the bridge, I could see it was an old wooden one with lots of holes in it and not very steady. Up on the slope, a party of men were coming down the track towards the bridge. The main in front was in Roman-style armour, a red cloak and with a sword by his side. "*Please, my angel, stay down here, but come to my call,*" said the Duke who walked onto the bridge, which clinked and rattled as he made his way to the middle.

As he did so, the party stopped on the other side of the bridge and the man in the red cloak stepped onto the bridge and walked to the middle to the Duke. The resemblance of the two men was striking as they met and embraced one another then stepped back to look at themselves and began to talk.

After some time, the Duke shouted something to the man and started to push the other man about to the cries of the men at the other side of the bridge. Then they started to hit one another with their fists, as men do. Then, would you believe it, they both drew their swords and to my horror and disbelief began to hit one another.

I was aghast at what was happening as the man in the red cloak did a vicious attack on the Duke who fell over onto his back where his sword bounced out of his hand into the river, pointing down the hilt upright. And then I felt a powerful force on my back and before I knew it, I had jabbed the standard pole into the river and with an agile leap landed in the middle of the two men, my cloak opening as I crashed down. I clasped with my left hand the sword arm of the man in the red cloak and I shouted, "STOP THIS!" As I landed the bloody sword flew out of the river and into my right hand. It was the same sword that got me here into this world in the first place and it thrust my arm up into the air and burst into flame and a blaze of light shot out of the tip up into the air, up into the overcast cloud cover and blew it away and bright sunlight shone down onto us all. Then the bridge gave way with a loud crack and we all plunged down into the river water.

As my head came up, I found the water was not too deep. I was only up to my chest in the chilly, cold water. Then we three just look at one another and all burst into laughter. After a bit, we all calmed down and I sat up and kneeled before the Duke. "My lord, please Caledfwich is not mine to use this day." Willing the flames to go out.

As he stood up to take the sword, the other man stood up and asked, "*Who is this beautiful creature?*"

The Duke said, "*This is my angel who gives me the means to take back my lands from King Vortigern by handing his sword to the Lady of this Lake. This my brother is Angelina of Heaven and of the Old Gods.*"

As I stood up my cloak and uniform heavy with water again, I bowed low to his brother and said, "I give you a good day, Uther Pendragon, you and your brothers' deeds will be sung by the bards for centuries to come and in books plays."

"*You know this for truth,*" he said, "*how?*"

"Ah, my lord, I have seen it with my own eyes. In my world, you have gone down into myth and legend. With your brother, you led the British opposition against the Saxons and helped establish a foundation upon which your son King Arthur is to build. Indeed you are both called the last of the Romans."

"*My son, but I have no son.*"

"Oh, you will have a son one day who will be Britain's greatest hero."

"*Come, let us get out of this river, my angel. Go and get dry, please. I will have words with my brother,*" said the Duke. So we all climbed out with help from some of the men. I left the pole in the river and I trudged back up the track, water sloshing in my boots as I went.

Up on the slope, somebody had lit a fire which I was glad to see. As I sat down onto a saddle, the Duke's men looked at me in some wonder as the winter sun warmed my back. After some time still drying myself off, I took Thunder Hoof for a ride up and down to dry the wet cloak in the wind and sun. After riding Thunder Hoof up and down, I rubbed her down with grass which was abundant on the side of the slope till she was glowing and gave her a peppermint to eat. Presently the

51

Duke walked back up the slope. *"Boys!"* he cried. *"My brother the prefect has given me leave to join him at his villa at Tintagel."*

"To horse!" he shouted so as I was by Thunder Hoof, I just mounted up and rode down to the river to the standard and I picked it up and urged Thunder Hoof over into the river. Of course, you can guess what happened next. The mad horse stopped in the middle of the river and began to splash me with lots of cold water. To lots of laughter, the Troop rode passed me up and over the river.

"Stop, you mad horse!" I cried. "I am wet enough already!" And to a loud horse laugh, she splashed out and cantered up the slope to the top.

So on to Tintagel, the Duke and his Troop with his brother's men rode up the hill together in a long column passing lots of what the Duke said were old tin mines of the old pagan inhabitants who traded with the people of the Mediterranean for amphorae, jugs, olive oil, wine from the old Merchant Venturers who went through the Straits of Gibraltar and up the Atlantic coast and the boats made the return journey loaded with a cargo of tin.

"Yes, in my world the tin mines were all over Cornwall in big, tall buildings with long tall chimneys."

"You do say some strange words, my angel, but then the Merlin said you were from a different time to the rest of us here."

"My lord, strange is not the word for it. I have seen one strange world and I come from an even stranger world than this but then I think you are the better for it."

"*Ah, if you say so, my angel, but if I had some tin ore to trade, I could pay my men and some men from Ireland to help me in my struggle as I have no gold.*"

"Oh, I met a troll who had gold but St Diana killed it, most horrible she was. She was going to take my essence, which Tam Lin gave me to defeat the Norn. *"

"*Ah, the Norns. The Merlin mentioned them to me. We call them the three fates, the Moirai, known to the Greeks who determined a person's birth, lifespan, a portion of good and evil and time of death.*"

"Yes, the Norn were a bit nasty to me but the sword was proof against the evil of the Norn, fortunately for me."

"*My angel, I have seen you do some amazing things so far but do not underestimate your power for you can do what I cannot do as yet,*" said he as he pulled the sword which Tam Lin had given to me he looked at me. "*When you landed on the bridge you made a big hit with my brother, you are unique.*" *Oh my god.* I *hate it when adults say these things to me,* it is so embarrassing to me and I was red in the face.

After about four miles, I could smell the sea and as we coasted a hill, I could see it sparkling blue on the horizon. The sun was still shining on this cold winter afternoon as I hacked down to Tintagel where I could see the island but no castle so I asked the Duke why there was no castle on the island. "*There is no castrum, as I call it, which means camp or fort in Roman Latin, my angel, only a monastic site on the island.*"

"There was a castle at Tintagel. I think the Normans built it after 1066 AD. Oh my God, not till 600 years' time or so."

"*Who are the Normans?*" asked the Duke.

"What, oh a people called the Vikings who settled in a place called Normandy. I read it in history at my school." With that, we rode to Tintagel, a good-looking hamlet with some stone-built homes, a market with what looked like an inn and a big villa we all rode into.

Then I see a big, white round tent in the distance. "Please my lord, can I be excused?"

"*Yes, of course, my angel, off you go.*" So with that, I urged Thunder Hoof into a trot over to the tent and as I dismounted Goewin and Brys ran out to meet me.

As we all flung our arms around one another. "E*ee, you are all damp,*" said Goewin as Brys stepped back.

I looked up at her in shock. "You can talk."

"*Yes, the Merlin has given our tongues back as we are now sixteen today and come of age.*"

"Oh, happy birthday to you both," I said giving Brys a kiss on the lips. "I am damp because old Thunder Hoof loves to splash me in lots of water." And Thunder Hoof then gave me a nibble on my back.

"*Ah, there you are,*" said the Merlin, "*I see you have upset the timeline again as there was no battle at Slaughterbridge. You must be careful as to what you do.*"

"Yes, sorry that I broke the bridge but it was that bloody sword again."

"*You will be careful next time. I am off to see the Pendragon.*" And off he went. "*Oh, get some rest. I want you tonight!*" he shouted to me.

"What does he mean tonight?" I ask Brys.

"*He has been down to his cave looking for something all day till the tide came in, looking very annoyed indeed all afternoon. But never mind, do come in and get warm.*" As he took Thunder Hoof inside me and Goewin headed for the kitchen for a bit of dinner.

Sometime later, I lay in a hot bubble bath my cloak, headdress and uniform hanging up to dry on the poles above the fire. Brys was sitting down with my leather riding boots, oiling them while Goewin was cleaning my school shoes and talking about how the sun had come out so suddenly. Then in walked the Merlin.

"You have the night off, girl. The weather will be bad tonight so no hope of you going down to my cave. I'll tell the Duke you are too tired to go to the villa tonight, so get some sleep, please."

"Good," I said, "I did not get much last night. Oh, by the way, Queen Mab is not very happy with you at all." And I raised my right arm to show the arm ring and Mab's ring of authority.

"Where has that come from? You saw Queen Mab last night? By the Gods, she moved far too quickly for my liking. What did you say to her?"

"Only that I cannot take off the arm ring till I reach Glastonbury. She was not happy to see red rubies in cold iron and I have to go what she called the Palace of the Thousand Pearls."

"Good, not much harm done then. All is well. So, good God, what is your school uniform drying for? Did you fall into the river or something again?"

"No, this horse of mine keeps on splashing me when I cross some water. She thinks it is funny." Then, from the back of the tent, there was a horse neigh and we all laughed loudly.

"So you be careful, girl. If you cross Mab you can be in serious trouble for she can be seriously bad and cruel and

horrible as she could be, but she is also the guardian who protects the world from things that were even worse than her, so go to bed."

Chapter 7

Day 9 – Merlin's Cave

The first thing I heard was the drumming of rain on canvas when I awoke in my nest of pillows and as I lay on my back I thought, *what day is it?* Ah, yes, it must be Tuesday by my recollection and, counting on my fingers, it must be what? Nine days ago, I fell down the water hole into the water hall and four days of swimming in terror out into this mad world and four days of riding on my pony.

Then I heard someone moving about in the tent and the Merlin appeared. "*Oh good, you are up I see. You can stay in bed as it is raining cats and dogs outside. The Duke is staying in the villa for some days to come so you can have some days off to recover from your riding.*"

"Oh good," I said turning over to sleep for some more time until the smell of cooking woke me and I rolled out of my bed to run to the loo.

A day off, *what can I do today?* I thought. *Ah, I know, I am going to wash my school uniform as I have worn it for many days and it must still be dirty.* So off to find Goewin, I went to ask her for some soap and a brush to clean and launder my blouse, socks, skirt and T-shirt and jumper, Mother's school tie and blazer and using the bath of hot water, I cleaned my clothes and inside my blazer pocket, I found the silver hammer the girl gave me with the silver links. I put it over my head for now and I was busy most of the day cleaning this and that, even Thunder Hoof got cleaned and buffed until she was shining. I even docked to the tail to stop it from getting mud all over it.

Then all was dry and clean and I got dressed in my uniform and began to stitch the dagger sheath into the inside of the blazer with the thread my mother had put in. After all was done, Goewin and I had a cup of herbal tea and then I heard it had stopped raining and looking out I could see mist and nothing else to be seen outside at all.

I had just sat down when the Merlin walked in all dry looking. *"Oh good, you are dressed. Please put on your boots and cloak and come with me now, we have two hours till the tide comes in so hurry up please."*

"Oh, okay." I got ready so on with my clean boots and then the blazer over my head with the cloak and turned to him. "Where are we off to?" I asked.

"Down to the cave to look for the Coat of Padarn Red-Coat. I put it there a long time ago and you can find it for me."

"What does it do?" I asked.

"It is the mantle of faithful wives which will cover the nakedness of a faithful woman but not an adulteress. The Duke needs it for his brother." And with that, I ducked out into the mist and followed him out into the gloom over the wet, soggy ground over to the cliff edge where the wind was cold and gusty. *"Come on, down to the bottom and be very careful going down, the wet stone path to the beach. Hold on to the ropes."*

Then he was gone. The path was very wet and on the very edge of a post. It seemed steady and reliable to hold onto so, carefully holding on to the rope, I made my way down to the beach step by step, hair and cloak blowing wildly till suddenly, all the mist disappeared and the wind went down and left me in bright sunlight and I looked up to see only mist above me. Then I saw I was only halfway down the cliff so I stopped and looked out to sea and I knew my home was just on the other side of the sea and with a tear in my eye I carried on down the steps.

"The tide is out," he said as I stepped onto the beach and made my way over to a big cave opening and I was glad to see no plastic bottle or rubbish of any kind, only driftwood and seaweed. As I stood at the entrance of the cave, I shouted hello and an echo came back to me, then a voice shouted back, *"Come in, girl, and put on these goggles."* So in I ventured into the dark cave to see the Merlin with a pile of sand in his hand with his staff lit up. As he handed me the goggles, he looked at the sand in his other hand and quoted, *"To see a world in a grain of sand and a heaven in a wild flower, hold infinity in the palm of your hand and eternity in an hour."*

"William Blake," I said.

"Very good, you know your poems. I have one more for you," he said throwing the sand up into the air. *"You throw the sand against the wind and the wind blows it back again."*

"Haha, you are very funny."

"Yes, Blake was a very funny man. I had tea with him once you know. Extraordinary man he was. Now on with the goggles and tell me what you see."

"Okay." I pulled my hood down and put them on. "What am I looking for?" I ask.

"A hidden cache. I put it here a long time ago."

"How long ago?"

"Oh, I cannot say with certainty, girl, so have a look around, please." With the goggles on, I could see what the cave was made of. I could see tin, gold and silver but no hidden cache.

"What does it look like?" I asked him.

"*A red robe rolled up into a bag.*" So for half an hour or more I searched.

"I have found a hollow over here," I said.

"*Good.*" He came over to me and put his hand in and pulled out the bag but it was empty. "*Oh, pooh, some sorcery at work here. It has gone.*" And with that, he sat down on the wet sand.

"Oh here," I said handing over the goggles, "I am hot in this cave and I am going out. My feet are too hot and it is stuffy in here."

"*Well, go for a paddle but do not go too far out there where is a ten-foot drop.*"

"Do not worry, I am not going to swim in that cold sea," I said walking out of the cave for a paddle.

Outside was very bright with the setting sun and I had to put my hand over my eyes to see where I was going. As I scrambled over the pebbles and rocks to the water's edge, I began to take off my cloak, headdress and boots and then my school shoes but they would not come off. *Ah, bloody stupid Merlin has put a spell on my shoes and I cannot take them off, oh well*. I put my things on a big rock nearby. *I shall have to endure wet socks and shoes, I supposed*. So in I splashed and sat on a rock and put my hot feet into the cold seawater to cool off, which was strange because I could not feel the cold water at all. So I sat and watched the big Atlantic waves roll in and swill in and about the rocks. It was very peaceful sitting down with the wind in my hair and in the sun.

I must have closed my eyes for some time until I heard, "*Look out, Angelina.*"

"What?" As I sat up the water was up my legs so I stood up to get out I saw a flash of silver out of the corner of my eye, there was a splash and my right hand was gripped in a forceful, powerful tug and before I could even scream I had tumbled into the sea head first into the sea foam, pebbles, driftwood and seaweed and I felt my knees being dragged over pebbles and rocks being scratched and my eyesight was blinded by seawater and stinging as I had always worn swimming goggles when I had swam in the sea.

Then I was in deeper water, hair and clothes flowing madly about me. My eyes began to clear and I had a good look at what was dragging me down to my doom. *Oh my God*, I thought as I looked. It is a savage, hideous-looking creature which had fins down its back and on its legs and arms which ended with flippers with nasty looking talons, bare-chested and female with long hair and fish scales with too many teeth for my liking and a big hooked nose and purple eyes. Then it stopped pulling me down and hit me in the chest with its flippers and all my air which was in me blew out and I thought, *is this my fate to drown in my school uniform, never to see my home or mother again,* as I swallowed cold sea water down my gullet.

A strange feeling came over me and I felt something in me and I did an involuntary spasm and hiccupped up a ball of blue water, forcing my mouth wide open, which made the creature swim back. Then more water flowed into me and I must have blacked out for some time. When I opened my eyes, I found myself drifting in the underwater current away from the creature who had an evil look in her eyes. *Hey, why*

am I not dead, then more blue bubbles flowed out of my mouth, *wow, quick, play possum and see what she does.* So I drifted lifelessly down to the bottom into the seaweed beds. With half-closed eyes, I wondered why I had not drowned. It must be the air spirit inside me keeping me alive, *oh good,* I thought. Pity I have to give it back.

Then the she-creature began moving toward me so I clenched my fist in my right hand then my shoes hit the sand at the bottom so I pushed up and did a right-hand fistful into the creature's mouth and it fell back. Then I made a break for it and stuck my shoes into the soft sand and pushed off the bottom but as I did so a flipper grasped my ankle and spun me back around to face her and we did an underwater fistfight and then it screeched at me and I felt a sonic blast which left me stricken. Out of the seaweed bed with an old-looking fishnet swam a bigger creature and I could do nothing about it as it began to wrap me up in the net with only my head and arms showing with my legs dangling out of the bottom. The small one let go of me and ripped up some seaweed and began tying it to my feet then with two more bits of long weed with that they both looked at me in wonderment as if to ask, *"Why are you not dead?"* They both looked at each other and screeched as if to say what do we do now. Then they must have come to a decision as they swam down and grabbed hold of the seaweed and pulled me into the depths. And the pressure underwater was getting to me as I have not been in deep water before, only on the surface and in rock pools.

As my head began to clear from what the creature had done to me, I noticed I was going back up then a dark opening appeared, it looked like a big underwater cave and both creatures swam into the darkness. For some time we all made our way up this dark passage, not that I could see it, but I could tell we were going up as the pressure was not too bad. Then I felt the creatures had stopped swimming forwards and I was being pulled up and I was spun around about in the net till I was free of it. My shoes were then grasped with great force and I was thrust up through the water. My head broke the surface into darkness and still being pushed up my body landed on a beach made out of seashells and I struggled to get a grip on the wet shells. With my legs still in the water, my body did a convulsion and my mouth opened wide and lots of seawater gushed out of my lungs, gasping for breath I spat out more salt water and gulped air into my lungs. The air was queer with a foul odour of death.

Chapter 8

Day 9 – The Sea Hag

Choking and spluttering water, I managed to crawl on my hands and knees out of the water to the screeching of the creatures behind me, my uniform heavy with seawater. The coldness hit me and I shivered all over with water dripping from my hair, I stood on shaky legs and trembled all over. "Argh!" I screamed as the cuts on my knees stung with pain from the seawater and I could feel the sensation of blood running down my legs, not good, as I stumbled forward hands out in the dark. And as my hands hit the slimy stone, my left shoe stood on what could only be bone as I stepped on it and crushed it under the heavy weight of my wet body.

"Bone!" I screamed. "I hate bones." And as I stepped to one side, *step-step*, *argh more and more of them*, I stumbled about until I stood on sand and pebbles under my feet and no more bones. I sank down onto my bum, my back against a wall and I brushed wet hair out of my eyes and whimpering in fright, I began to cry and sob in pain and fear. Being very cold and wet, I tugged up the collar of my blazer to the back of my neck and tried to fasten up my blazer but my hands were too cold to do them up so I clasped my hands together and bowed my head down into my chest and pulled my throbbing knees up.

I was sitting down shivering for some time, spitting out bits of sea water from my sore painful throat and feeling wretched as my jaw was painful and aching from coughing and from the sickening smell of something long dead. A sinister laugh echoed in the dark and I could sense something had moved toward me and heard on my left lots of screeching from the creatures, which echoed around what must be a big cave or cavern. "Who's there?" I called out, my voice hoarse as I pulled myself up on shaking legs, my back to the wall, arms out for balance as I edged my way back from the awful voice that echoed around the cave.

"*Itss speaks, itss stillll aliveee. My childrensss 67ys haveee 67yse 67, there 67yse beee aaa 67yse bonusss forrr 67ys alllll.*"

"Stay back," I croaked in my painful throat. As I edged away, my foot crushed bones again and in my panic crushing more bones I was flinging my arms about when my right hand hit the side of my sodden blazer and I felt my dagger sheath inside.

"*Noeee whereeee to hideee, myy sweettt, youuu areee minee to eattt, youurr head 67yse beeee senttt 67ys trollllss forrr paymenttt, aahhh haahhhh.*"

Quickly, my left hand pulled out the dagger, my right holding the bottom of the blazer and as it came out, it lit up the cave and in front of me was a disgusting creature, I screamed in some fear and horror. It was a green she-creature with two legs with fins, all covered in seaweed on her arms and legs and wearing a ragged torn yellow dress with a necklace of finger bones.

I TODD P

A W L

She had wicked-looking webbed hands with hideous long claws, black eyes and a hooked nose and black hair. "Oh my God, what is it?" I cried.

"*Sea hagss weee areee. Yoow aree myyy prayyy, my sweettt, wee will eatt 68ys and the crabbeses 68yse haveee your bonesss to eatt. The trollssss want 68yse headdd, myyy sweettt, 68ysel 68yse beee muchy merriement inn theirrr realmmm 68yse II brinngg them your headddd.*"

"You–you want my head," I croaked as I put the dagger into my right hand.

"Youuu kill troll queen, whichhh trollsss 69yse revengeee onn youuu, my sweettt."

"I did not kill the witch, my school icon, St Diana with the sword of light did so there, you hideous old hag," I croaked.

"Hideousss amm, III haveee youuu seen yourrrselfff, landdd dwellerrrr, yourr virginal angelic, pure selfff iss filthyyy too mee anddd yourrr puny knifeee 69yself harmmm meee inn this realmmm." And with that, the hag lashed out at me with her arms and I ducked down just in time as her claws raked my hair and I thrust upwards blindly with my dagger with my right hand and hit something hard.

The shriek she made was deafening and then I was hit in the chest and I was sent flying backwards in the air and landed with a thump, fortunately, on soft sand and pebbles but I was winded. My chest hurt like mad and it was hard to take a breath so I lay listening to the she hag screeching and I must have passed out.

After some time, my breathing was better and so I sat up to see the she hag was doing a dying fly, arms and legs in the air then she lay still with my dagger in her mouth. *Good and I need my dagger back*, I tried to stand but I began to tremble all over so lay back down and wondered where the creatures in the sea cave had gone to as all was quiet. With much effort, I rolled over onto my front and began to crawl my way over to the hag and pulled out the dagger from her mouth. The dagger's light lit up the cave too bright for my eyes to see until they become better used to it and looking around, I could see a dark opening at the back of the cave. I crawled as far away as possible from the hag, put the dagger in my left hand and pulled myself up the wall with my right hand very slowly, legs trembling in fear as to what I had done to the hag but it was either live or die. Holding on to the slimy stone, I slowly made my way over to the opening I had seen and as I looked at the sound of gurgling water, the notable fresh air hit me in the face. It was the only way out. I had no desire to go back down the dark tunnel I had come up in and it was the only way forward.

My bloody knees had clotted by now but were still sore and I forced my way down the tunnel hoping there were no more sea hags down there. Then the light hit water slowly coming towards me and I knew the tide had turned and was coming in. I must get out so in I splashed, the water around my feet, then my socks, my knees and then to the hem of my skirt. Holding on to the side of the tunnel, I could see lots of anemones, ragworms, mussels, limpets and winkles all on the walls of the tunnel with lots of seaweed hanging down from the walls and I could feel the flow of the tide against the material of my school skirt pushing it back around my knees then up to my thighs. I struggled on until I was chest-deep arms out in front of me then I saw a passage on my right-hand side. Something glistened further up the passage as I looked in but did not stop. As I struggled on for a bit more, the flow of water was running too rapid for me to advance any further with the incoming tide.

The water was now up to my face and I could tell I was not going to make it out so I had to turn back. As I did so, the flow of water picked me up and I was pushed back up the tunnel. I managed to grip some hanging seaweed which was horrible and slimy and I was swung around in the current until I saw the passageway I had noticed before on my right. I let go and swam over and into it still being pushed along by the flow of the water, but not too bad. My shoes hit stones and I was able to stand up, chest deep in chilly sea water and holding up the dagger I saw a long passage reflected in the dagger's light. Moving on, the water level went down to my thighs and I splashed on around a corner to be greeted to my amazement by a hoard of treasure which glistened in the glowing light of the dagger. "Oh my God!" I cried. "A king's ransom!" And gawked, my mouth open at the sight of diamonds, rubies, gems and jewels and lots of gold coinage, coffers and chests all in a pile on top of a high ledge above sea level.

As I stood in shock, my legs shivering with the cold, I hooked my right leg up and with my right arm pulled myself over the top to see a dry alcove at the back with some dry seaweed which could be a bed of some kind. As I stood dripping seawater out of my uniform, I looked at all the pile of gold and I thought the Duke could do with this lot for his troops but how do I get it to him?

I looked into the bed of seaweed and examined it for any more hags but fortunately, it was empty but putrid so I left it alone and tried ringing out some seawater from my uniform and looked at my scratches as I sat down. *Not too bad*, I've had worse falling out of a house but still very sore. As I rubbed my knees the blood had all washed off by now. I sat and watched the tide coming in but to my relief, it did not top the ledge and being all cold and wet I would have to stay in this refuge until the tide goes out in six or more hours' time. Being too tired to move after being kidnapped by mer creatures, almost drowned and then had to fight a sea hag, I was in some discomfort as to what the sea hag had said to me about the trolls and the troll witch. I will have to tell the Merlin all about it. As I sat, I wondered to myself whether it was a waste of time washing this uniform as it was all now sea-stained then my head just sunk down in my exhaustion and tiredness and I fell asleep.

Sometime later, I awoke and found myself lying down on my side by the wall with my dagger still in my hand and a salty taste in my mouth and my tongue was on fire. I need water but not sea water but I had no choice but to roll over into the water. Once in, I hoped the Air Spirit would not let me drown as I gulped in sea water and as before a big blue bubble rose out of my mouth. *Ah, much better*, now I was under water and by the light of my dagger, I could see the water was lower than before.

At last, the tide had turned which meant I could swim out of this horrible cave but first I must grab some gold so out I climbed onto the ledge and spat out all the sea water after some coughing up and had a good look at all the hoard of gold.

The gold coins will be too heavy to carry so I opened up one of the chests. *Oh ho, look at all this*, it was full of pearls, lots of them. Next was a coffer full of rings, chains, bracelets and necklaces and in the big casket was one red robe, ah ha. I bet this is what the Merlin was looking for so the nasty sea hag had found it and put it with all the gold so he would not be able to find it, so he had me go down to look for it so the hag had only to wait for me to go to the sea for a paddle.

So what? Does the Merlin want me dead? For as I thought he wanted me to get to Glastonbury so he could get into the sanctuary? Oh, he will be disappointed, won't he? As I thought about it, I spread out the red robe and filled it up with rings, pearls, bracelets and some coins and gold chains then I thought I will have three necklaces, one for me, one for my mother and dad so around my neck, under my school jumper

I put them so they would not be seen. With that, I tied it up with two gold chains and tested the weight with my right arm, *not too bad now let's move and get out of here.* With that, I jumped in only to find I was only knee-deep. Good, so I splashed down the passage.

Chapter 9

Day 9 – Selkie

It was then my toe hit something underwater and I fell down head-first into the water. "Bah," spitting out the water I reached under to see what I had fallen over to reveal an antique box with ivory all over it with figure drawings and runes like I had seen on the troll bottle. As I picked up the box, I found it to be very heavy for a small box and I opened the box inside was lots of small, twisted gold rods about an inch long. *Oh, more gold.* As I was about to drop them back in I had a brainwave. I picked one out to see if it would fit one of my school skirt plaids. Yes, it does so I filled up my blazer pockets as much as possible with the gold rods.

Dropping the box back in, I splashed my way back to the main passageway to see the tide was going out at last as the seawater was running fast out so I untied my dagger and held it up for light for about five minutes. On I go, on down holding onto the walls for five minutes as the cold water was now up to my waist and I waded into a big sea cave and I could see light, yes, yes.

On my left side was a big opening out to sea with large waves breaking onto rocks with spray and I could see sky and clouds. *Oh my God, how long have I been down in this cave?*

To my right was a smallish opening where the seawater seemed to be flowing. So that is my way out, not to swim out to sea as it would be hard to do. As my dagger lit up the cave, I could see a ledge dropping down to rocks in front of me so I took a deep breath and ducked down underwater to see how far down it went. I could see some big rocks to my right but it was clear below me with only pebbles and small stones. So here I go again. I put my dagger back inside my blazer as I could see where to go by the light from the opening. I went down onto my knees, left hand on top of the ledge, right hand with the bag of gold and pushed off the ledge and dropped over to the bottom. As I did, I opened my mouth wide to let in seawater and the big blue bubble forced its way out of my mouth and with the weight of the gold and my wet uniform, I sank down so fast my school tie flew out of my school jumper as I hit the bottom and I had no time to put the damn thing back in as the water current dragged me off my feet and I had no choice but to go with the flow.

Now as I have said on this matter before, school uniform is not meant to be swam in and with shoes on, it was especially hard with an open blazer as well and it was all I could do to keep myself off the bottom as I was propelled forward at some speed. Swimming on with the current pushing me up this tunnel with the flow, I saw a big opening up ahead and daylight. At last, I can get out of here and hopefully I swam up. But as I was pushed out of the tunnel a side current hit me and I was spun about into a kelp bed and oarweed forest. As I tried to swim out, a very big grey seal shot out of the kelp forest in front of me and I did an underwater scream. In my panic, I cast my arms back and kicked for buoyancy. The big seal did not swim off as I expected it to but hung in the current with no difficulty at all but looked at me with some intelligence in his black eyes and as I tried to swim up, it thrashed its tail and thrust itself at me. Then I was grasped by its big flippers around my head and it put its nose into my ear and a male voice shouted, "*Follow me if you want to live!*" Well, the startling revelation of a talking seal was new to me but then I have heard and seen a lot of weird and bizarre things to date.

As the seal hit me, I was pushed backwards, legs and skirt flying forward as he/it then let me go and dove into the kelp forest. I did my best to follow the seal but was still being spun about. It flew out of the kelp and swam next to me and put its flipper into my left hand which I grasped and we shot into the kelp forest where I was lashed by lots of kelp and all I could do was close my eyes and hoped it soon stopped. After a while, no more kelp hit me and I opened my eyes to see we were in a clearing. The seal pushed me down to the bottom and as I let go of the flipper, he/it put he/its mouth into my ear. "*Stay here.*" And was about to swim off then put his mouth into my ear. "*Push your hair down.*" And then he was gone.

As I sank down, the current was still alarming so I dropped the bag of gold and grasped a root of the kelp with my left hand, down to my knees, right hand on top of my head to keep my hair down and with my school tie and skirt flowing about me, it was hard to stay down even with the arm ring of Mabs giving me the strength of ten men. This was most strange, who has heard tales of talking seals? I raked my mind for stories about them and as I did, he/it swam down to me and he/it put his nose in my ear. "*Hold on to my tail now.*" So I let go of the kelp and grasping the bag of gold, held on to his/its tail with both hands and with a swirl of sand and pebbles with a flick of his tail we glided up with no struggle at all. As he swam up, I could see more seals darting in and out of the kelp as I flew through the water and now I could see the surge of the waves and they were big ones. *My God, how far am I out to sea?* The noise was deafening as we got near the top. Then the seal flicked its tail and I lost my grasp on it and I began to sink down with my weight of gold and wet school clothes and I tried to swim then I saw the seabed was now much closer than before.

Then suddenly, the seal was back and he gave me his flipper to hold onto until we hit the surface of the waves and I could see the swell by the coast some way off so I sank my head down into the waves then the seal was gone. I let the swell force me onto the beach until my shoes hit sand and pebbles and my feet slipped on the slippery sandy shore. I seized a handful of sand and scrabbled out with the tide's help up onto the beach where I was horribly sick as all the seawater flowed out of me. I shivered with the cold now that I was out of the sea and I felt so tired and wretched as I wheezed more water out of my mouth. Then I heard a crunch of pebbles and a shadow fell over me and I looked up to my side and saw a pair of legs and heard a gruff voice say, "*Be you, the angel, everybody is looking for? You do not look like one and what have you been doing in the briny deep at the hag's cave and wearing funny-looking clothes, hard to swim in? Good job, I found you before the hag's girls got you or you would be fish food by now.*"

"Who are you?" I cried out of my very sore throat and I gasped sea air into my lungs.

"Please do you have some water?"

"*Water,*" he said, "*I just pulled you out of the water. Do you want me to put you back in the sea, my fish girl?*"

"No, no, water to drink," I croaked.

"*Oh, why did you not say so.*" And with that, he picked me up by my arms and flung me over his shoulder and walked up the beach. I felt as if I were a sack of potatoes as he ambled up the beach and he bumped me along. I was able to spit out more seawater. Good job, I still had the bag of gold in my hand. "*Here we are, fish girl,*" he said as he slid me back over his shoulder. There was water running off from the cliffs above me and I put my head into it and quenched my thirst with lovely cold, tasteless rain water.

Then the fatigue of two days with no food hit me and I felt sluggish. I must have passed out for I found myself in the arms of the man who now was on top of the cliffs and I heard lots of voices. "*Look the selkie has the Duke's angel.*" Selkie, oh now I remember that is the name for shape-shifting seal people who have the ability to become human and leave their seal-skins concealed somewhere. Then I was carried over to the villa much cheering of "*Angel, angel, he has found the angel*" and out ran the Duke who embraced me and then stood back as I was still all wet and I gave him the bag of gold.

"*Where have you been, my angel? You have been gone for two days. The Merlin said you had walked into the sea and I can tell by what you call a uniform that you have been as you are all wet.*"

"Huh, I was dragged in by some hag creatures down to be eaten by a sea hag and my head on a pike to be sent to the bloody trolls!" I cried to him. "But look in the bag, my lord." His eyes went very wide as he opened the bag of gold. "There is a big pile of gold down in the hag's cave," I said, "and I had to kill her." It was then that I realised I had broken the Lord's commandment not to kill. I had not thought of it until now and I fell to my knees on the floor sobbing and crying my heart out. I had killed!

"*Quickly get my angel to the Merlin, he will know what to do with her,*" the Duke said to his men.

As I was carried away I was croaking, "No, no he sent me to the hag." And I was crying all the way to the white tent.

79

Chapter 10

Days 10–18 – Sick Days

As we all got to the Merlin's tent, or yurt as he calls it, the flap flew up and out ran Goewin and Brys. "*By the gods what has she been doing now!*" cried Goewin.

"*We will take her, argh she is all wet.*" And in a haze of pain and still sobbing I was carried into the tent where I was stripped out of my wet uniform and then I began to tremble and shiver with cold so, coughing and sneezing, I was lowered into a hot bath. As Goewin began to wash me, she cried, "*Oh, look at your chest!*" It was all covered in blood with six claw marks all on the front of my chest from where the sea hag had hit me in the fight and it was all red and inflamed. It was at this point I passed out only to awake to find myself in a camp bed sometime later with a bad cold or flu with a bandage around my injured chest. Thunder Hoof was looking at me with confusion.

"Hey," I croaked to her and she neighed.

"*Ah, the patient is conscious at last,*" said the Merlin who was standing by my side. "*You gave me a big scare, you were near death, my girl. If it were not for Mab's essence in you, you would be dead and the Air Spirit would have turned the sea blue to survive. What possessed you to take on a sea hag, you crazy girl?"*

"You tricked me," I croaked. "You said to go into the sea for a paddle. You knew the sea creatures were there."

"I deny it. I did not know the hag's girls were aware of your presence in this time frame but I knew the robe was missing by sorcery by something out of this world and with your unique abilities you could find it for me."

"Ah, you knew the sea hag was there all the time. The bloody hag was to take my head to the bloody trolls and eat me," I said choking.

"What," he said his eyes wide. "The trolls sent the hag to find you? This is too mad. How did the trolls know you were here in the first place?"

"I do not know," I croaked. "Water please."

"What, oh, here you can have this bottle of cold water."

As I drank the nice cold water, he said, *"You do know every time you use that dagger you got off the Otter God, it grows one more inch every time you hit something out of this world. It is a side effect of being put next to Excalibur."*

"Please do not remind me of that silly sword, it was what got me here in the first place, was it not?" I cried.

"I suppose so but it must be how the trolls knew you were here. The sword is of Fay's work and its power reverberates throughout the realms of existence so it must be how they found you and sent the hag after you."

"Great, but what did the hag do to me when she hit me in the chest?"

"That is how you got poisoned. You were lucky that your school blazer, lining, jumper, blouse and underthings took

most of the blow so some poison did not go into you as it was all wet."

"Did that mean I could not breathe for some time afterwards as I must have passed out for some time? Was it the poison in me?"

"Yes it was and you gave Goewin a big fright when you fainted in the bath. Brys had to hold you up as Goewin ran down to the villa to find me. I have cleaned your scrapes and grazed on your knees but you will have to stay in bed for a week at least for your chest to heal."

"Ah no, please listen. I have sinned. I have killed. I will go to hell as I had to kill the horrible hag so I am doomed to go to hell. I have broken the word of God not to kill," I said crying.

"Ah ha, oh ho, you crazy girl, you have already been there, silly girl. Did you not find yourself at the bottom of the Yggdrasil, the world ash tree, and did you not escape on your own, from the fiery Hel."

"What, do you mean there is more than one?"

"Well yes, Hel is an old Germanic word for hidden place and the name of the Norse Goddess of Death."

"Oh yes, I have seen her at the Norns' well, not nice I thought."

"What, you saw the Queen of Death and she let you go? Good grief, girl, what are you, some sort of demigod's offspring?"

"No, I am not but Queen Mab said I was of the ancient lineage of somebody called Bran the Blessed, whoever he was."

"You mean Bendigeid Fran, the giant of ancient mythology who gave up the cauldron of life, death and

inspiration, the life-restoring cauldron to the Irish when he had to wade across the Irish Sea leading the British boats to defeat the Irish."

"And what happened to him?" I asked.

"He had to rescue Branwen, his sister who married the king of Ireland but he was mortally wounded in the heel. His men had to cut off his head and buried it under the White Tower in London as he was the guardian of Britain."

"That is what Mab said."

"Yes, it is why they have ravens at the Tower with their wings clipped or will have some day, for Brans' name means Raven. Ha, did you say you killed the hag? Gods, I will have to tell the Duke. Oh, by the way, thanks for the red robe of Padarm Red-coat, now go to sleep."

* *
* * * * * * * * * * * * * * * * * * *

The next thing I knew was Goewin shaking me awake. *"Please Angel, eat some vegetable soup."*

"Hello," I croaked my throat still very sore, "what time is it?" I asked her.

"Oh morning, you have been asleep for three days, Angel. Please eat some soup, you need your strength. The Merlin has been to the Duke and they want you to go back down to the underwater cave where you killed the sea hag."

"Three days?" I croaked to her.

"No, not again, not with the sea hag's girls down there," I said as Goewin fed me the soup. Sometime later, when Goewin was giving me a wash, I asked her what happened to the gold I had in my blazer pockets.

"*The gold rods and necklaces are in your blue bag under the bed. Brys discovered it in the blazer and concealed it before the Merlin saw it and the necklaces I took off of you in the bath.*"

"Oh, thank you. I was going to sew them to my school skirt at the bottom of my pleats to stop it flying up as I ride Thunder Hoof. Oh yes, can you ride her please?"

"*I will do if you do not mind.*"

"Please, if you would. She needs her exercise but do not go near water."

"*Haha.*" Goewin laughed. "*Yes, I know,*" she said as she finished washing me.

As she left, I pulled back the bedcovers to see my knees had mostly healed from the seawater, which happens to cuts, it must be the salt but it did hurt. As I lay back, I looked at my chest bandage and I felt it gingerly. "Arghh!" I cried out. "That hurt."

Goewin ran up to me. "*Do not tear your bandages, Angel, it will be some days before they may come off.*"

"How long?" I asked her.

"*I think you will have them on for four more days yet. Here I have this.*" And she poured some water into a wooden cup. "*Now drink this, please.*" So down it went and at once I felt queasy and I settled down to sleep.

I awakened in the dark and I felt somewhat better, a lot better than before. My throat was not as sore as it had been and I needed to relieve myself badly and so I got out and as I stood up my hair touched something. Feeling above me I felt my school blazer bottom, which was hung up so I felt for my dagger sheath and pulled it out, which lit up my surrounding nicely and I put my blazer on for warmth. I wondered what time it was. All was quiet. *Where is everybody?* So with some effort, I made my way to the loo and sat down for some time until I needed some air. I made my way over to the opening and took a good deep breath of night air. Ah, nice cold air down my throat which then made me cough as I still had a bad nose cold and looking up, I could see the Cosmos, the night was clear and the Milky Way was an amazing sight.

Then a voice said, *"Hello, fish girl, what are you doing out of bed at this time of night?"*

"Oh hello." And I held up the dagger to see who it was. It was the Selkie who stood there looking at me. He was wearing a brown tight tunic with bare legs. "Are you not cold?" I asked him.

"Me cold? No, fish girl. Us Selkies do not feel the cold but you do, standing there in silk underthings and what the Duke called a blazer, but you must be."

"What!" looking down at myself.

"Ah yes, do come in and have some tea."

He looked at me. *"What? In this small hut?"*

"Oh, do come in, it is not a small hut at all but a big tent so do come in, please. I do wish to thank you for helping me."

And with some disquiet, he entered into the tent and his eyes went wide and he cried out, *"Wizard magic!"*

"Do not worry," I said. "It is only a spell to hide the tent, which the Merlin calls a S.E.P.F. spell."

"And what does that mean, fish girl?"

"I do not know as yet as I have not worked it out but it will come to me in time. Yes, you can walk around this tent without seeing it." I walked over to the cooking area to light up the fire with the magic word Goewin was teaching me to say but my throaty voice made it too difficult to distinguish what I was saying so I had to do it with some matches from my bag and I made some herb tea for us. After sitting down with the Selkie I asked him his name.

"Bodcoccus, fish girl," he said, *"and as I said before you were lucky."*

"Lucky?" I asked him.

"Well, do tell me."

"Well, fish girl, I was in the kelp bed looking out for the sea hag when you swam out and I was going to wallop her with my tail when she swam out but it was you and I had to stop myself from hitting you, fish girl."

"Oh, I see. But what were you doing there in the first place?" I asked.

"The hag and her hag girls were eating all my clan's fish and all the other fish had gone away so you see why I was hiding, fish girl."

"Your clans. How many of you are there please, for in my world you are only legendary."

"In our world, fish girl? Where do you come from?" he asked me.

"Let me see," I said as I counted on my fingers. "It is 1520 years' time in the future and I live in a very strange world, for where I come from there are no Selkies at all."

"No Selkies!" he cried out, jumping up.

"No." And then he ran out of the tent. *Oh my God, I have upset him now,* I thought.

Two minutes later, Goewin ran in and the lights lit up. *"Oh, it is you,"* she said. *"I saw a light on. Oh, you got the fire going. Who was it I saw run away?"*

"It was only the Selkie, I think I upset him."

"You did, how?"

"I told him there were no Selkies in my world and he ran out and where is everybody. It was dark all around when I woke up."

"We were all down at the villa celebrating Imbolc, the Celtic start of spring. Sorry, but you were asleep. How do you feel by the way?"

"A lot better, thank you. How long was I asleep, please?"

"Six days so far."

"What," I croaked, "I've been in bed for six days?"

"Yes, you had to heal the wound on your chest, which meant you had to keep still for some time. Let me have a look at you. Please take off your jacket and hold up the nightdress. Ah, not too bad. The swelling has gone down somewhat so I will put some cream on it. Hold still, please." After some time and with some food in me, I went back to bed for the rest of the night and most of the next day until the Merlin had a look at the wounds and did an examination on me and declared me free of poison. As Goewin unwrapped the bandages, I could see six holes where the claws had gone into me on top of my chest and no wonder it had hurt. Then she put some healing salve on my chest and I was able to sit outside in the sun for some time for my health.

The Merlin sat down next to me and asked me if I was willing to go back down to the sea cave and bring up the rest of the gold for the Duke as the Selkie had run off. "That was my fault. I told the Selkie that there were no Selkies in my world that I know of and he ran off."

"By the gods, you do have a talent for upsetting people, do you not?"

"Yes, but do I have to go back down to the sea cave with the threat of the sea hag's girls still down there, as the Selkie called them?"

"Their name is Fenette or to you, Nixies. They are adept shapechangers and can transform themselves into fish or mermaids but they have now gone away as you killed their mother."

I looked at him. "You are positive they are not there anymore as I would not like to meet them again."

"I can say they are not there anymore but the sea hag had to get here somehow so I would like you to find the portal to the parallel world where she must have come from and close it down if you could."

"How?" I asked him.

"I have a gem which will close the portal. All you have to do is place the gem inside and it will collapse. Plus, it will be good for you as the trolls cannot find you again so quickly."

"You mean they will try again?"

"Well yes. If they find you here, they can find you again so it would be for your benefit and with your ability to breathe underwater you are the only one who can do it."

"It is not very pleasant with seawater in my lungs. It is only the Air Spirit keeping me alive as I am its host."

"Pluck, girl, pluck is all you need. Tomorrow there is a low tide when you can swim out to the cave entrance and be out before the tide turns, plus the seawater will do your wounds the world of good."

"Ah, I would like to do something to my school uniform before I go back in. Could you ask Goewin to bring out my bag and school skirt, please?" All afternoon Gowein and I sewed the gold rods to my school skirt pleats to keep them weighted down, I hope.

Chapter 11

Day 18 – The Portal

The next day, I got up and put on my now revamped uniform with the gold rods all around my skirt and the blazer bottom. There were a lot of them left over so I gave the rest of them to Goewin and Brys for helping me. The necklaces, I put inside my bag.

As my chest no longer hurt, I found Thunder Hoof's harness and reins but not my saddle and slipped out before anybody saw me. I found Thunder Hoof in with all the mares in a pen. When she saw me. She ran over to me neighing like mad. As I kissed her, I slipped on the reins and harness. "Do you want a run?" I asked her, she neighed to me. Good, so I opened the gate and led her out through the gate. I sat on her back and rode her backwards and forwards to see if the rods all around my skirt were working. Yes, they were to some extent which was good so I put her into a gallop to the way I had come days ago and it was working but I will have to see what the skirt did on my saddle. So back into a trot, I turned her back towards the pen I had found her in first only to see the Merlin waving to me from the tent. So, turning her, I trotted over to him.

"*You must be a lot better if you can ride your pony. Come in with the pony.*" And he opened the tent flap as I slid off Thunder Hoof and led her in. "*The tide will be out in a bit and I want you to be ready to go to the cave so put on your blazer with the dagger of light just in case you find something down there in the dark. But have some food, my girl. I do not want you to pass out again and here is a good breakfast, so eat it all up.*" I remember my mother said the same thing to me what, more than two weeks ago. Oh my!

After breakfast, I rubbed down Thunder Hoof and fed her, put on my blazer and made sure the dagger was inside the sheath. As I was putting on my blazer, the Merlin said to me, "*Here take this reed basked with you as well.*"

I looked at it and said, "It is too small to hold all that gold and boxes. There is lots of it down there."

"*Ah yes, but it will hold it all and will also float the stuff and it will help you swim out as well.*"

"How will it?" I asked.

"*Girl, it will help you so please hold on to it as it will home onto the gold.*"

"Oh, so it was a magic basket then. Tam Lin had a magic tree which gave me food and drinks some days ago."

"*You ate the food of the Fays. You mad girl, you are now bound by Mab for all time.*"

"Yes, I know. She explained it all to me, what she wants me to do for her about eight days ago, I think."

"*You crazy, girl, do you know what she can do to you? She will enslave you.*"

"No, she will not. I have to do one job for her in what she calls the bottomless deep to get the air spirit out of me safely."

"Hmmm, girl, it may be so but be careful with your dealings with Mab is all I will say to you. Now, if you are ready, come with me down to the sea. I have made it calm this day for you so you will have no difficulty swimming out to the headland."

"Why to the headland?" I asked.

"The cave entrance is just below the headland. I will guide you in."

"How?"

"I have my ways, girl. Oh, yes take the goggles as well. The portal may be hidden from view."

"Where are they?" I said as we walked out of the tent.

"Here." And he pulled them out of his robes and handed them to me. *"Do not lose them."* We walked to some steps going down to the beach he said, *"There you ago, be careful going down as there is no rope on this one."*

"Are you not coming down with me?"

"No, I will be upon the island. See you." And he vanished in front of me! I will never get accustomed to that happening to me, crazy wizard.

Holding on to the walls, I made my way down feeling the strange weight of the gold rods all around my school skirt bumping against my knees. I hope it is worth it. As I made my way down onto the shingle, I wished I did not have to swim in my uniform again but Merlin's spell on it gave me no choice in the matter. As I stepped onto the sand, I saw the waves were not very big and with cloudy skies; it looked all right for a swim. So in I splashed up to the knees then around the hem and then I heard a shout to my left. As I looked up, I saw the Merlin pointing out to sea and I did the finger up to him as I waded in and this time; I was going to keep my mouth shut and have no mouthfuls of seawater if I could help it. With the water now up to my middle, I dove forward and swam with the basked on my right, which was hard going so I stopped swimming and put it into my left hand and with some trepidation, I struck out into the cold Atlantic waters, my right arm working to keep my head above the waves and with the basket in my left hand, I found I was swimming in circles so had to stop now and then to correct my course.

After some time and with some effort, I got to the headland so I looked up to see the Merlin pointing to my left side so, waving to him, I took some deep breaths and dived down to see an underwater cave and I could see it was the cave which I was pulled into by the hag girls and I hoped the Merlin was right in that they had gone away. The basket then began to drag me into the dark cave so I hung onto the basket and I pulled out the dagger to see where I was heading only to see lots of sea weeds waving with the water current. Then with a rush, my head broke the surface into the cave I had been to before and I took in some air and began to climb out not looking at the body of the hag or the bones and hurried on past feeling cold and clammy and shaking water from my head, I began to walk down the passage I had gone down before.

* *
* * * * * * * * * * * * * * * * * * *

It was a lot easier to walk down the passage with no seawater coming in but the stones were slick with weeds and tricky to move over. Then I saw water in front of me but not too deep, only knee high and so on into the passage which led into the treasure cave. And it was all still there glowing in the light of my dagger and the basket was jumping up and down in my left hand so I threw it over the top and climbed up the ledge only to see the bloody basket was on top of the treasure pile upside down in some enjoyment and it gave me amusement to see it over all of the gold pile sucking it all up, gold and the boxes as well.

As I stood up, I put on Merlin's goggles and had a good look around when there was a thud and the basket flew up and landed upright and all the gold and the boxes were all gone. Well, well, it was a magic basket all along. Oh well save me doing it so I began to look for the portal Merlin said was here somewhere and at the back by the seaweed bed was a big box with lots of gold and green work on it, very nice to look at with a big lock on it and it had not been there before.

As I walked over to it, I could see the gold was in a coiled form of an octopus and I knelt down by it to look at the lock with the goggles yes, there were octopi all over the box with scrolls. Ah, it must be inside the portal then. So I pulled on the lock and then wished I had not done it. As I put my dagger down in the sand, I opened up the lid and put my hand into my blazer pocket for the charm the Merlin gave me and then, *Wham,* the lid shot out of my hand and a very horrible-looking tentacle with a nasty-looking hook on the end of it appeared out of the box and shot into the air. I must have been startled for some time as the tentacle got longer and longer out of the box and as I jumped up my hand in the air, the goggles fell off as I made a dash for the passage. But then I was enveloped by the tentacle and I struggled to free myself but I was then drawn tight around my legs and I was yanked suddenly into the air. The tentacle tightened around my body and head first

I was pulled into the box. I screamed. I had no time to pick up my dagger as I plunged headlong into darkness only to have a face full of warm blue water. Water, *oh no more water*. I had no breath left in me at all so I opened my mouth wide and in flowed not sea water but fresh drinking water. As before, a blue bubble burst out and this one was bigger than before. *Boy, that hurt*, then this blue water began to clear and I saw a humongous-looking octopus.

Oh my God, look at it, at least 50 feet around with tentacles to match. As I was pulled down, I could see a very long beak. *No, no, it is going to eat me.* When I got to its mouth, the tentacle spun me around and I saw two big black eyes looking at me. *"Hag, hag, where is my box?"* a very loud voice echoed in my head.

As I found my buoyancy blue bubbles flowing out of my sore jaws, the voice said, *"You are not the hag, where is the hag, little one? Tell me now or I will eat you."*

Now in terror and awe, I shouted, "No, no, I am not the hag, she is dead. I had to kill her," but as only bubbles came out of my mouth, I was afraid it did not understand me.

"What, you killed the hag?"

"Yes, it was live or die. Please do not eat me." I thought, *where have I said that before?* "I will be horrible and tasteless!" I shouted at it.

"You killed the hag. What will become of my children?" And with that, the tentacles flew up as in a sorrowful distress and I was spun about madly till I was seized hold by a tentacle and pulled down to its face.

"You killed the hag, how little one?"

"By my magic dagger of god slaying," I shouted, "I stuck it into her mouth."

"You, little one? How is it possible, she was a powerful sorcerer?"

"Yes, I know, she was going to take my head to the Trolls."

"So you are the one who is behind why the hag kidnapped my children to force me to give up my box so she could go to your realm."

"Hey, it was not my doing. It was my patron the Goddess Artemis, who killed the witch troll, not me, now the trolls want my head on a plate. It was they who sent the hag after me," I shouted back at it.

"Be that as it may but now I have no way to save my children as the hag put them into a cave and I am too big to get them out."

"If you let me go, I will find them for you if you would, please."

"Why would you do this thing for me, little one? You look too weak to me to do anything to me."

"I'll have you know that I am the champion of Queen Mab, companion of Merlin the wizard and Uther Pendragon and the Gods of Asgard and holder of the magical sword Excalibur. I will find your children for you."

"You will, how?"

"You said the hag put your children into a small cave. Am I not small enough to get into this cave of yours? But first, I need my magic dagger, please."

"You said you had the sword, Excalibur. Even I have heard of it in my time, little one. Where is it?"

"At this time, it is in the hands of the Lord Uther Pendragon. My dagger is its companion. It is up in the sea cave," I said pointing up to the portal as I was madly treading water.

"And I am to get this dagger for you is that it? You would use it on me to escape would you not?"

"On my honour as a good Christian, I will not kill you this day."

"A Christian. I've heard of Christians. What do you do?"

"What do we do? We worship the One God Almighty."

"The One God, I know four of them myself, little one."

"Well, they cannot be very good can they if they let your children be captured by the hag, can they?"

"Careful, little one, you never know who is listening."

"Yes, well, I met three myself. One I had to kill to get my dagger, who was an otter god the troll witch said who was captured by the evil Norn."

"It was you who sent the Norn back to her sisters. That was a mighty task indeed, little one."

"Ah yes, but it was the sword that did the job. I was just carrying it for Mr Tam Lin who was in a tree of life."

"Alright, little one, you have convinced me. Will you help me to free my children?" And with that, it shot a tentacle up into the portal and came down with my dagger which it/he/she dropped before I could catch it which was strange as there was no water resistance at all and I shot past my dagger with ease. Stopping was no fun and the skirt hit me on my nose as it flew up as I grabbed my dagger.

"*Come, little one.*" And a tentacle twisted around my waist and I was dragged along at some velocity into the blue waters.

* *
* * * * * * * * * * * * * * * * * * * *

"Where are we?" I ask it/he/she as we shot along.

"*In the head waters of a very big lake, little one. Up ahead is a labyrinth of caves in which the hag put my children somewhere so I could not reach them.*" Before long, a crack emerged out of the blue and a hole loomed up far too small for it/him/her but big enough for me to squeeze through. As we stopped, I could feel the flow of water out of this hole then the tentacle shoved me into the hole and propelled me up through a small passage into a big opening which my dagger lit up to reveal an underwater cavern. Then the tentacle thrust me up and my head broke the surface into the cold air and, shaking the water from my eyes, I could see lots of stalactites and stalagmites. Then the tentacle let go and I began to sink down under due to the flow of water from somewhere. So I had to pump my arm and legs madly to get up to the surface again. I managed to grasp a stalactite to hold on to and had a rest then all the water in my lungs burst up and I had to spit it all out of my mouth.

As I scanned my dagger about, I could see an opening on the other side with water flowing out of it so I swam over to see if it led to anywhere. Letting go of the stalactite, I had to do the crawl stroke to get to the opening, it was not easy in my heavy wet clothes. And then my shoes hit bottom and with much effort, I pulled myself up and began to wade up the opening up against the flow of water which swirled my skirt around my legs and I had to use my hands to keep upright. Pressing on the water began to get lower, now down to the bottom of the skirt and then I could see a solid door made out of glowing crystals. As I went to open it a spark flew out onto my dagger and made it flicker and sparkle. *Oh no, you don't,* and I hit the door with the dagger and the door shattered into smithereens and I was covered in splinters.

Oh well, that went well. Then I had to jump out of the way as a hoard of octopuses flowed out of the hole where the door was. It was easier to go with the flow back into the water and out into the blue waters where the big octopus was covered in children, a happy sight to see. *"You did it for me, little one. I thank you and now I will let you go."* And with that, it wrapped me in a tentacle and we were off back to the portal. *"Go now, little one, and can you shut and fasten the lock if you would,"* it said as it unwrapped me. I said I had a gem to close the portal and I pulled it out of the blazer pocket and held it up for it to see. *"Now that will do, so fare you well then, little one."* And with that, I kicked my legs and shot up into the portal where I had to grasp the sides of the box and pull myself out, dropped the gem into the box and it disappeared.

With that done, it was time to head off back to the tent to dry off. As I turned around, I saw the basket had moved over to the edge on its own, *mad thing.* Right, let's go and I jumped into the water. It was deeper than before and was up to my chest. Oh no, how long have I been in this water world? It did not seem long to me at all. I pulled the basket into the water and it began to move off on its own. As it did, I remembered the box under the water and I grasped it as we shot over it and with my right hand hurled it out of the bottom into the basket.

Out in the tunnel the water level was high so the tide was in and almost to the roof but this time the magic basket was in charge, so grasping the sides of the basket we started off into the cavern and the basket turned left and headed for the open sea. *Eek! Where is this thing taking me?* One deep breath and I ducked my head as the roof of the cave shot over my head and up I went only to see an iron boat bobbing up and down with the Merlin inside. "*Where have you been?*" he shouted to me as the basket hit the side.

"*You have been gone four days now so up with you?*" And the basket and I rose out of the sea and dumped into the boat, *ouch*.

"*What have you been doing now?*" he asked me as I lay on my back looking up at him and gasping in the cold air.

"Me, oh I had to help a very big octopus rescue its juveniles held captive by the sea hag," I said.

"*And the portal? What happened to it, did you close it?*"

"Yes, I did." I sat up and looked about me as it was my first time in a row boat out at sea. Oh, I have been on boats before but they were big ones.

"*Here, wrap yourself up in this.*" And he handed me a robe, which I gratefully wrapped myself in from the cold and gripped the sides of his rocking boat. He then said some words and pointed his staff and the boat moved off in the direction of some big cliffs. "*The Duke had to move to Warbstow Hill Fort two days ago to see to the troops. He is having to pay for to restore his kingdom and it is where we are going to with this gold you got me. We must go to the port of Boscastle and into an opening in the cliffs.*"

We arrived at a port full of big boats and a fishing village in a valley basin with a river valley running up to the hills beyond. I saw the welcome sight of a white tent up on one of the hills and asked him, "Why is it up there?" as we moved to a jetty.

"*I will tell you later on so come on.*" And with that, we walked up to the tent with the gold.

Chapter 12

Day 22 – St Nectan's Glen

Back in the tent after a hot bath and cup of tea and a bite to eat, I went to bed for the rest of the day only to be shaken by the wet nose of my pony sometime later. Thunder Hoof was so pleased to see me and with that, I got up and hugged her nose and she gave me a wet kiss. "Hang on, you mad horse, I have to get to the loo first then we will go for a good ride, so out of my way, you mad horse." Having got dressed in a dry uniform again, I put on the saddle and pulled down the stirrups to see if I could ride with a straight leg for once and see if the skirt would keep down.

I did not go far as the Merlin saw me leading out Thunder Hoof. *"There are still wolves out there, my girl. I would hate to see you being eaten by a wolf."*

"Oh, but really wolves out there?"

"The last wolf was killed in the fourteen hundreds somewhere up North."

"Good grief, a thousand years of wolves to contend with. Well, I hope I will not see any of them today. If I do, Thunder Hoof would outrun them, won't you, girl?"

As I led her out the Merlin said, *"Go down to Nectan's Glen and go to the hermitage as it will be called one day.*

There is a nice waterfall to look at. Just follow up the glen to it, you will be delighted by it."

"How far is it?" I asked him.

"Oh, not too far, just follow down the road till you see a nice little wooded valley and go up the path and on your left have a look at some ancient rune cut marks on a rock face."

"All right, I will go and have a look." And I did up the saddle and girth but not too tight, on with the bridle, made sure the blanket was over the loins and putting my foot in the stirrup mounted up. I had to stand up to tuck in the skirt, not the best thing to ride in as you know but then I had to make the best of it.

Off we trotted down into Tintagle Village and all the villagers looked at me as I rode by so I gave them a good wave. I saw some woods on my left side and found a path and on we went into a gallop and, yes, the gold rings all around my skirt were working as it did not fly up so much as before. With a boom-boom, Thunder Hoof was living up to her name as we made our way down this road to the woods. The Merlin said there was a waterfall and yes the road led down to a dip with a sloshing little stream which led down into a very rocky valley and the road went up a wooded hill. So turning Thunder Hoof to the left, I let her go up the stream, which she was delighted to do. It was very warm down in this valley of rocks so I was glad I did not have my cloak on.

A little way down, I noticed an overhanging cliff with lots of long weeds hanging down over a dark, wet patch so I had a look and on the flat surface of the rock were cut two spirals so off I got. "Stay Thunder Hoof," I said to her and had a better look at the runes. *My, my, very old Neolithic*, I thought, very nice rock carvings that must have taken a long time to do. Oh well, so back up on Thunder Hoof, I turned her around and rode back the way we had come. Over the road and up the wooded glen, we went following a well-used path by the flowing stream all the way up until I heard a waterfall. As there was no way up for Thunder Hoof to go, I tied her to a tree. "I will not be long up there," I said to her.

As I looked up, I could see a man standing on top of the waterfall and he shouted down to me, "*You girl, come on up! I would like to see you.*"

"Who are you?" I asked but he had gone away.

As there were lots of outcrops, it was no effort to climb up to the top without getting wet, where I found the man in the water up to his knees. "*Come here, girl, and let me look at you.*"

"Who are you?" I asked him.

"*I am Nectan. I give you greetings. I am the guardian of all the waters in this land. My queen has asked me to see to you to be clean, pure and white.*"

"Oh, nice of you." I backed away I looked up and there before me was at least a 60 ft. waterfall, all with green rocks which the water had punched a hole through into a big pool.

"*Come here, girl.*" And as my shoes were in the water at the time, he held up his hand and all the water I was in rose up and I was raised up and it began to move me over to him.

"What do you want with me?" I cried to him as I struggled to free myself as I floated over to him. Then he took my hand and pulled me over to the pool. It was then I noticed he was walking on top of the water.

"How are you doing that?" I cried.

"Girl, I am a water deity. It does not mean I have to get my feet wet now does it my girl so stop your whingeing." And with that, he cast me into the cascade.

SPLASH! I found myself on my knees in cold water again as I tried to get up but he held me down. *"Calm down, girl, this is holy water. It will clear you of all ills and diseases that the evil sea hag did to you and restore the essence which Queen Mab gave you as it kept you alive for this long."* So as I had no choice as to what this man or god was doing to me. I let him do what he had to do to me, which somehow took some time and I was glad I was getting used to cold water, then he pulled me up. *"Well, all done, my girl. Now go for a swim in the pool for me and catch three young salmon, who must have followed me over from Ireland and who have been eating my hazelnuts of wisdom."*

And I stood up dripping, looking at him. "You want me to do what, catch salmon. How can I do that?" I asked.

"With this." He pulled out a three-pointed long fork. *"With this, and then we can have them for lunch."*

"Oh good. I am a bit hungry." So I took the fork and as I was already drenched waded in up to my middle, took some deep breaths and dived in.

As the floor of this pool was full of pebbles and with no weeds to speak of, there was nowhere for the salmon to hide in. The last time I had fished was in the waterfall cave some time ago. There was a flash of silver, I put my shoes to the bottom and pushed up after it and with some force, I shot over to the fish. The fork impaled it at once and I looked back from where I had come from. Wow, I must have travelled underwater a good ten feet in what two seconds and with that I pulled out my dagger and hit the salmon on the head as I had done with my dad when we had gone fishing in the sea. Right, two more to go. Funny this water was no longer cold but very warm so it was a pleasure for once to swim in even in my uniform, which I have had far too much practice as of lately.

So I pushed off the bottom with my shoes to look for the other two and with no time at all, I had swam buck up to the surface and waded out up to him with three salmon on the fork. To my amazement, there was a setup fire-dogs and a fire going, two stools, a bowl of greens and a keg of some kind and I handed the fish to him. "*Good, you did very well under the water in what Mab said was a uniform. You can swim with no effort at all, which will see you good when you go to the bottomless deep and it is good you can hold your breath for some time as you were under for a good half hour.*"

"Pardon me, but did you say a half hour? But that is impossible," I said to him as I stood dripping water out of my uniform.

"*No, it is not with me in with you at the time to see how you did. Now come and sit down by the fire, girl, do not get too cold. I hope you like fish and you are dripping water onto dry stones, which will never do.*" And then he pointed with his finger at me and all the water on me ran off me into the pool, leaving me all damp so I was grateful to sit by the fire. In no time at all, he was cooking the salmon and I wondered how I had been under for so long without air as I had not swallowed the water at all, so strange. Then he gave me a mug of mead, which I drank down at once.

As he sat, all the water flowed all around his feet and I looked down to see, yes, the water was up my legs and I had not noticed at all but not the fire as it was in a little island of its own which was funny to see, then he handed me my fish with what I think was watercress with some seasoning. Very nice to eat but I had to use my fingers. After I had eaten my fish and washed out the bowl, I had one drink of mead. "*Good. Now you have eaten my fish of wisdom you will be able to understand all that you hear spoken to you and the speech of animals, birds and fish but not reptiles as they have not a good word of anybody so do not bother.*"

With my eyes wide I said, "You mean I can talk and speak to my pony? Oh, thank you." I cried as I jumped up and splashed my way over to the edge of the waterfall.

I look down at my pony who looked up at me and said, "*It is about time you showed up.*"

I must have squealed in joy as the man held my arm. "*Now hear, my girl, Queen Mab will be pleased to hear you have been healed to be able to get to Glastonbury so my work here is done, so goodbye.*" And he walked over to the pool and dived in and all his pots and the fire was gone as well.

Oh God, I do meet some weird people in this world. I will be glad to go home. I made my way down to where I had left Thunder Hoof and as I was getting cold due to my damp clothes it was nice to get back onto a warm pony. Now I wished I had bought my cloak to go over my wet clothes to keep me warm, oh well never mind. Turning Thunder Hoof back the way we had come, I turned her to the right and up and around and up to the top of this hill to a level road with hills on my right and the sea on my left side. So I let her have her head and we galloped along at a good speed, *boom-boom*, behind us till we reached a big deep valley where I reined her in and had a look down to what looked like a harbour with lots of boats. Ah yes, it is the port of Boscastle down there.

Right, let's go back so I turned around and trotted her all the way back to the rocky valley and let her have a drink then back up the hill and on to Tintagel and by now I was almost dry but the breeze off the sea was cold so I rode to the tent where I gave her a good rub down, some feed, checked and cleaned out her hooves. Then Brys led her to the horse pens and took all the horse gear into the tent where the Merlin looked at me. *"Have you been swimming in your uniform again, my girl?"*

"Well yes," I said. "I met a water god who held me underwater for some time and he gave me more essence to get to Glastonbury and when am I going, please? I have missed up to three weeks of school work already and all my friends, school and my mother. I would like to go home, please."

"Yes, all right. I know you are homesick but get out of your wet clothes now and have a hot bath please and some rest, for tomorrow we will all go to Warbstow Hill Fort to the camp."

"Good," I said putting my saddle on the pole and then Goewin helped me out of my uniform and into a hot bath, which was lovely after a long ride but as I had eaten a whole salmon, I was not hungry at all. So off to bed with a hot cup of tea, I settled down in my sea of pillows and went to sleep.

Chapter 13

Day 23 – Warbstow Hill Fort

"Get up sleepyhead." And I was tickled on my right foot. I looked up and the Merlin was standing there with a mug in his hand and a roll of bread which he gave me. *"Do eat up and get dressed as the yurt is coming down today. We are off to see the Duke so get up, girl."* So after my food and drink, I was up and in my uniform, now dry again, and looking forward to a day's ride on Thunder Hoof to a camp of some sort – not too far away I hoped.

Merlin put the yurt down with his staff and as he did, it turned into the ramshackle hut I had seen on my first day in this mad world, then he *swam*, the hut onto a big-looking cart which had no horses to pull it at all which looked ridiculous only to me. With Goewin and Brys on top, it began to move on its own down the road into Tintagel – what a sight to see.

"Right, on your pony, girl, and follow the cart if you would please."

"How are you going to get to this camp?" I asked him.

"Walk it, my girl, now come on."

"Okay."

As I mounted up Thunder Hoof neighed, "*You do know he is as mad as a hatter?*" And I did a good belly laugh and almost fell off my pony.

"*What are you laughing at, girl?*"

"What, oh something she said." And he gave me a look as if I was as mad as he was. So off we went all day and by the afternoon, it began to rain so I was glad I had my cloak on with the funny old helm on my head as I did not get too wet for once with my long-riding boots. On and on we pulled up a very long hill up to a very used track, which led up to some hill where in the distance, I could see something like a high hill which must be where we were going. So looking around me now the rain had, at last, stopped I saw some cows, funny-looking brown four-horned sheep with lambs and farms dotted here and there. Then the sun came out and it was quite nice with all the water on the hedgerows all dripping and shining bright in weak sunshine and all around me, there was green grass everywhere. This really was no wilderness but a very orderly land.

And on and on, up and down valleys and hills till I could see smoke on the top of a high hill and as we approached, I saw lots of men with hammers and saws putting up a palisade of some sort. Then there was a trumpet call and they all stopped what they were doing, all stood up to see us and looked at the horse cart with no horses to pull it. Out of one of the gates came a troop of horses, which thundered down to us and pulled up in front of us and there was the Duke and Mr Pendragon on big horses with stirrups made of wood, very crude but steady looking.

"*I am happy to see you, my angel, and you too, Merlin. Welcome to my fort. I hope you will be happy here. We must have a feast tonight in your honour for the chest of gold jewels and the robe for which I thank you."* And with that, he leant forward and kissed me on my lips. Well, I was in shock as I had only been kissed by my dad before who did not count and I did not understand why he kissed me. *"Do come up to the fort, my angel, and see what you have done for me,"* he said. Then we all rode up and into this big hill fort with three ramparts with circular huts and one big hall on top of the hill.

"Come with me," said the Merlin taking my horse reins in his hand and leading me over to the site where the tent was set up in the lower ring it being bigger and as the man on the walls looked on the cart stopped in the middle and the Merlin held up his staff and the hut jumped off the cart and instantly turned into the yurt.

"You still living inside that old hut of yours?" said the Duke who had followed us into the lower ring.

"You are all invited to my hall tonight where I hope you will sing for us, my angel, as there is a feast in your name tonight so do not be late."

"I am going to put my pony into the stables over there," I said to the Merlin and I turned her head and got off and led her into some warm stable. "Here, have some dry hay." And I gave her some to eat with some of last year's dry oats I found in a trough.

I thought that it was still fresh but Thunder Hoof tucked in and said, *"Nice, last summer's oats, nice and tasty."* So as she ate I gave her a good rub down with some dry hay, took off her harness, saddle and reins and cleaned them with the oil from my saddle bags, combed out her tail with that Saxon bone comb which was as good as anything I could find to do it and with the curry comb I did back, loins, chest, legs, flank and lastly the forelock.

By this time, I had taken off my cloak, headdress and boots as well and was sitting on the funny helmet the Merlin said I had to wear when I heard the sound of hoofs on the soggy ground outside then boots hitting the ground and a female voice said, "*You silly horse.*" And into the stable came a young girl, no younger than me leading a big-looking horse, all black with no saddle at all. The horse was a bit high-strung, excitable and skittish and about sixteen hands high. "*Oh,*" she looked at me in the darkness of the stable "*Are you one of my lord's hirelings, girl? Put this mad horse into a pen for me.*" As I stood up, the sun came out and shone through the door of the stable, revealing my scarlet uniform and blue plaid skirt and black socks and modern school shoes. As I took the reins off her, I saw she was in a yellow riding dress with a gold belt and long dagger sheaf and red fur-lined cloak and she had a gold ring on her head.

"*Oh my,*" she exclaimed when she saw me in the light, "*You are the angel my lord said was coming here today.*" And she dropped to the ground and bowed her head to me.

"Please do not," I said as I took her hand and she looked up. "I am Angelina of Swansea or Abertawe," I said, "and I am not an angel but a girl out of time and lost in the Dark Ages as the Victorians will call them, but do stand up if you would, what is your name my lady if you would."

"*My name is Igerna. I am betrothed to my Lord Gorlois, Duke of these lands all about. I am to be wed in two days' time. I hope you will be in attendance as I have heard you can sing like an angel.*" And in shock and astonishment, I know who this girl was, *good grief*, she is the mother of King Arthur and I could see she was a great beauty and of good stature and of high station.

"*She is a pain in my back.*"

"What?" And I looked at the horse I was holding by the reins.

"Haha. He just said you are a pain," I said as I led him to a horse pen and tied him.

"*You understand the word of horses? You are in truth an angel and of the Lord God and we are blessed to have you in our company. Please come with me up to my bower and we can see if I can find you a nice dress to wear to my wedding, my angel.*"

"Alas, I cannot take off my school clothes as the wizard Merlin has put a spell on it so that I cannot take it off."

"*Oh no matter, but please come with me up to the top of the hill. I will show you the best place to see the countryside. You will need your cloak as well as it can be very windswept this time of year.*"

So I put the cloak and headdress back on and saw Thunder Hoof was alright stuffing herself silly on hay and oats. "You will get fat you will," I said to her giving her a pat. And following the girl, we ran up through all the gates and passed all the men who were working on them at the time who just looked at us and laughed as we were both in giggles all the way to the top. There, we both pulled up our hoods as the wind was a bit cold but it had blown all the rain clouds away to reveal a view of green hills and forests all shining in the light of the setting sun. The only clouds I could see were on the horizon out to sea.

As she sat down she said, *"Please, Angel, can you sing me a song of your home realm as I would like to hear one Christian song this day, if you would please?"*

"Yes, okay, what would you like to hear first?*" And I sat down on a dry piece of ground.

"Something good to light up my day."

"Right oh.*" So I sang her some songs which I knew she would like to hear and she closed her eyes and smiled in pleasure to hear my words and we sat and sang until it got too cold to sit anymore. Saying goodbye to the girl, I ran back down to the stables which were all black so I had to pull out my dagger to see if Thunder Hoof was okay only to find her fast asleep in the light so I carefully covered her up with the blanket and tiptoed out.

Back in the yurt, Goewin was cooking some food when she saw me. *"The Merlin is looking for you,"* she said, *"where have you been?"*

"What, on top of the fort with the Lady Igerna who will someday be the mother of one of this country's greatest warriors, who will drive back the Anglo-Saxons for years to come." Just then, the yurt's flap opened and in ran the Merlin.

"By the gods, there you are. Where have you been, my girl? The Duke is looking for you, he wants to take you to be his wife at the wedding and that cannot happen and he wants a son to rule after him."

I just looked at him. "But I am too young to get wed, I am only 14 years old."

"Ah, don't you believe it, my girl? You are the perfect age in this timeline to be wed. Look at mad King John, he kidnapped an 11-year-old girl who was on her way to be wed and made her his Queen."

"But-but."

"No buts, girl. Go and get all your belongings together now, we will have to go tonight but first, I will have to do some big magic on the fort so we cannot be seen leaving, so go now."

And out of the tent, I ran back over to the stables to get my bags and wake up my pony who was still asleep on her feet in the hay stall. "Wake up, my pony. We have to go tonight." And I began to pack up the things in my saddle bags.

Chapter 14

Day 23 - Pursuit

As I was putting on the saddle, Goewin ran in with some bags. *"Here is some food for you and for your pony. I think it is goodbye as the Merlin is going with you. He told me and Brys to go back home."*

"Oh, I am so sad to see you go, you have been a good friend to me ever since I have been in this world. Would you say goodbye to Brys for me, please?" And I embraced her with tears running down my cheek. Then good old Thunder Hoof gave her a lick on the face as well and we both laughed. *"Goodbye, sweet girl."*

"Oh, she said goodbye to you," I said, "give her a pat." And then I took the food and placed it in my saddle bags. "Farewell, my friend," I said as Goewin ran out then the mist rolled in through the stable door. *Strange*, I thought, as it was quite thick. I finished putting the tack on and with my cloak and funny helmet, I led Thunder Hoof out only to see mist, mist and more mist.

My goodness, you could not see a hand in front of your face it was so thick. As I walked forwards I shouted, "Hello, is anybody there?" then a hand grasped my arm.

"Come with me, girl, now." And out of the mist was the glowing tip of Merlin's staff. *"Come with me, girl, the mist will hide us as we leave. Pull the pony along but keep her quiet if you would."*

"You heard the man, be quiet, my girl."

"Do you want me to go on tip-toe? Because I cannot, I have hooves you know."

"Oh, all right, just try and we may be able to get out."

"Who are you talking to, girl? Do be quiet and we will be out in no time so follow the light. We must get through all the gates." I could feel we were going downhill and suddenly there was no mist.

"Right, my girl, get on your pony and ride to the port of Boscastle. Go down this hill till you hit a river bridge then turn left and follow the river up the river valley until you come to a road or track and head downhill. I have a boat waiting for you. I hope you do not get seasick." And with that, he vanished.

So up on Thunder Hoof, I rode down this hill in the dark wondering what is going to happen to me when I got to the port of, *what did he call it?* Boscastle. It was then I hear a horn blowing and as I looked back over my shoulder; I saw a fire arrow arc up out of the mist followed by more of them. "Oh great, we have been missed already. On, girl, on," I called to Thunder Hoof. By pale moonlight, we went pell-mell down to a track which led downhill until we came to a ford in the track, both ways leading downhill. "Great, which one? Oh well, the left one." So off we galloped and as we shot down a steep incline, I noticed on the right side a dark-looking valley and on the left an even bigger one. I must be on a ridge of some kind and then the track levelled out and I saw lights on my right side and dark shapes were visible on the track in front of us.

"On, girl, on." And we shoved our way through them and I saw they were only shepherds with staffs and three men jumped back as we shot passed with lots of cries of alarm, "great, now we have been spotted." Then the track went downhill some more and in front of me, I could see more lights in the distance someway off and, with shouts behind us, Thunder Hoof galloped on down till I saw water glittering in the moonlight where a ford and then a track appeared on my left side. I could see I was in a deep river valley with a river running down into darkness. Slowing down Thunder Hoof, I gave her a pat and put her into a walk as we got to the ford and I turned her to follow up the river valley into darkness.

Into the river, we splashed. Fortunately, the water was only a foot high with Thunder Hoof loving it. As we made our way up, I had to duck under trees and brushwood, which loomed out of the dark and I was not going to use the dagger of light to see as it would give us away. After some time, I heard a trickle of water on my right side and it being dark under all the trees and bushes, I could not see which way to go so I dismounted into the river but fortunately, my riding boots kept out the cold water. "Keep still, Hoof, please."

"All right." I splashed to the opposite bank over slippery stones and grasped a nearby tree and hoisted myself out and, *bang,* my head hit a big dark tree. Oh was I glad I had on the helmet the Merlin gave me and I now see the advantage of wearing one.

I pushed myself through some bushes and looked to see where to go next. Over to my left, I could see fire torches moving down the track I had come from. Goodness, they were quick and I could see the ford from here. I watched as they stopped for a bit then they moved off up the track away into the darkness.

"Good, they are gone." So looking up the valley, I could see where to go and back in the river, I splashed over to Thunder Hoof. "Come on, they are out already looking for us." And taking the reins, I led her upriver. Moving on for some time, the valley split into two but the water was deeper on my right and it seemed the correct way to go. Up and up through this dark valley we went till it levelled out, the river now a small stream, and in the light of the moon I could see some bracken in a long line, it may be the track the Merlin said to take. On the top, I had to stop and take a deep breath and despite the cold winter's night, I was sweating with water running down my back, not nice at all, after climbing up the valley. "How are you, Thunder Hoof?" I asked my pony. "Can you run at all?"

"All night if I have to, my girl."

"Right, come on then, we need to find a way through this bracken and find the track down to the port." So up to the bracken, I pulled her. The bracken must have been five or six feet high.

Then I heard voices on the other side of the bracken wall. "Sshh." I put my finger to my lips to Thunder Hoof who gave me a funny look. As I listened to the voices, I could not make out what they were saying at all but at least four men were on the other side so I sat down and listened to the voices as they faded away into the distance. I stood up and pulled Thunder Hoof to the side and began to look for a way through. "Come on, Thunder Hoof, I can see an opening in the bracken here." Somebody had made a hole through and I led her in. I looked both ways only to find a mud track leading uphill with lights on my right going down to a hamlet. So which way, up or down? As I knew there were some men up ahead, I got back on Thunder Hoof and quietly we made our way up the track till the track split into two. *Hmm, which way?* In the moonlight, the track led away on my right up into darkness but the track in front of me led uphill, so on up I urged Hoof, up the steep track.

On I rode up until the track levelled out at a cross track with a little one in front of me but on the big track, I found myself leading downhill and I could sense the sea was close by so I chose the track going downhill. As we turned toward the downhill slope, I heard a shout and looked about me. I saw some men sitting down in the dark by the side of the track. "*Stop, stop!*" they all yelled as they leapt up next to me and tried to stop me from going downhill. One of the men tried to grab the reins out of my hands and the other two men began to pull me out of the saddle but the fourth man made the mistake of going behind the back of Thunder Hoof who went suddenly mad and kicked the poor man flying with a yell of pain. Then she bit the man who was holding my reins and spun around so fast I almost lost my seat as my cloak was ripped out of the hands of the two men who leapt back in some haste when she screamed loudly at them.

The effect was terrifying for me and the men began to run for it as fast as they could run, leaving the man who had been kicked lying in the mud groaning. For a while, we both sat still in shock until I heard a horn blowing someway off. "Come on, Thunder Hoof, we must go on down to the harbour before the men come back for us." And we turned around and made our way down the track at some speed. As we passed a track leading off on my left, I saw a group of horsemen with torches come up the track toward me.

"Good grief, here they come!" I cried. "Go, go, Thunder Hoof." And with a loud neighing she took off at a gallop down the track with the horsemen in hot pursuit and I was glad I was on an Asgard pony with, *boom-boom,* thunder claps behind us as she was faster and surefooted as the ground was soft from the day's rain.

"*Stop, stop,*" came the sound of the Duke calling to me but I paid no attention to it. As I shot down, I leant forward as I did not want an arrow in my back. Down, down we went flat out leaving the Duke's troop well behind us. Then around a corner, the harbour came in sight and in the dark I could distinguish a large throng of men who were in a fierce and savage fight with what looked like Vikings to me who were holding back some men with a shield wall of spears.

In the harbour was, and I am not kidding, a big Viking ship with a ramp down one side and then I saw a light being waved on board the ship – it was Merlin with his staff! Good. As I turned Thunder Hoof to the ship the shield wall gave a big cry and began to push back the men and made a gap for me to ride through. "Go, Thunder Hoof!" I cried to her. And she went off, *boom-boom*, went the sound of thunder as her hooves hit the dry ground and we flew past the shield wall and what I think were Vikings gave a great shout as I thundered passed them onto the ship.

We thundered up to the ramp and with one great leap, Thunder Hoof cleared the side of the ship and landed on the deck only to slide to the other side of the deck and as she tried to stop, she lowered her head and I was shot forward over her head and was catapulted over the side. As I flew over, the side my helmet came off and I hit the water headfirst and down I sank to the bottom and as I was in full school uniform, cloak and boots it was hard to find some buoyancy as there was an underwater current. Then my feet hit the ground and I could see the ship's keel was no more than a foot clear of the bottom, which was full of long, green weeds. I tried to swim up but the current dragged me along the bottom it was then I saw a big-looking wooden rudder which I grasped and with Queen Mab's arm ring of strength I pulled myself up to the top and my head broke the surface. Gasping for air, I spat out a mouthful of seawater and with my cloak trying to drag me back under I yelled, "Help, help!" Two big men looked over the side at me and they lowered a rope to me, which I grasped and I was pulled up out of the water.

When I was near the top, I hooked my left leg over the edge and with some strength, I was pulled over the side of the boat and was helped up by two fair-haired men who looked at me and then began to laugh at my sodden appearance and as I struggled out of my wet cloak I said thank you to the two men who pulled me out. They stopped laughing and said, *"How is it you know our speech, girl?"*

*"*What?" I said as I stood there water dripping onto the deck. "What do you mean?" I said, beginning to freeze and shudder with fright from being launched overboard into the cold sea. "How can—" Then the night was lit up by a big ball of light from the bow where the Merlin was standing throwing balls into the air over the heads of the men who were fighting the shield wall, which broke up and ran back to the boat. Not listening to the two men, I began to scramble over benches, seats and oars back over to Thunder Hoof who looked at me and gave me a horse laugh.

"You look like a drenched rat, my girl."

"Well, thank you very much," I said as I began to tie her up to a nearby post and seeing her body was hot to the touch, I covered her up with my wet cloak over her loins and loosened her girth strap.

The men who had been in the shield wall clambered onto the ship and took up oars, after putting down all the shields and spears and began to push off the bank but the last man to jump on board was a big man in the ring mail armour with a boar-headed helmet with gleaming cheek-guards and hand axe who began to shout at all the men with the oars. As I looked at him, there was a clang as the two men who pulled me up dropped an anchor and a swinging cable on board and the ship began to drift with the current away from the bank.

After one more ball of light at all the men who were crying, *"Come back."* The Merlin walked up to me.

"Gods, you are all wet again."

"Yes," I said, "I fell overboard when Thunder Hoof landed on the deck and I shot over her head. Oh, I am sorry I lost the old celt helmet, it fell off my head into the water."

"Ah, well not to worry too much. It will be in some old musty museum one day. Here, come with me, girl, I will get you a warm cloak to wear as it will be cold out at sea." Just then, the man in armour came over to us.

"Is this the girl we had to wait for, wizard?" He looked at me then at Thunder Hoof. *"Was it worthwhile to have my men wounded, wizard?"*

"You will be well paid for holding back the Duke's men, Ormson Halfdane. You and your men came off lightly in that fight due to my magic. Now this girl is Angelina of Asgard and that pony is also from Asgard, her name is Billey Thunder

Hoof after one of the Valkyrie's horses which can fly. Her sire is one of Odin's spirit flying horses."

The look of wonder on his face was great to see then he took my hand in his and said, *"Welcome to the Raven, my Valkyrie, but you look a bit young to be one."*

Chapter 15

Days 23 and 24 – The Sea Raven

"Yes, I am," I said, holding on to the Merlin's line of the topic of discourse, "but we have to start somewhere, do we not?" I said to him as I gave Thunder Hoof a fond pat on her neck, which was still steaming hot from her run down the hill.

"Ah, yes it would seem so. But what are the words on your chest?" And he bent down to look at my blazer badge and he mouthed the words *"Truth and Justice"* from the Latin motto of my school blazer pocket, which was still wet and shining in the torchlight. Then as he stepped back from me, *"Gods, girl, you are all wet."* And he pulled off his warm cloak and put it around my shoulders and I thanked him for it draped around me *"Welcome to the Raven, girl."*

I remembered my manners and bowed to him. "It is my honour to be on your ship this day and I give you my blessings on your voyage my Lord Ormson Halfdane." Just then I heard a horn blow and I looked over the bow of the ship to see the Duke on his horse with all his troop of horses all around him and I could see all his men begin to get ready all the boats up on the side of the harbour.

"Ah!" cried Ormson Halfdane. *"He will be lucky to get those boats in the water as the tide is turning in our favour."*

And wielding his axe he brandished it in the air and then began to shout at his men, *"Out oars and keep her off the rocks."*

As I looked about me, I could see we were drifting passed some high cliffs all dark and menacing but the men with the oars knew what they were doing in the dark with the help of the moonlight. As I watched the cliffs go by, I turned to the Merlin. "Who are these people?" I asked him. "And how did you know they were in the harbour as I could have got lost in the darkness for some time and missed you completely if it was not for my pony." And I looked at Thunder Hoof who with her legs locked was fast asleep.

"Ah, well, you see I knew Ormson was in the harbour at this time as he has been trading up and down the Irish coast. He and his men are Geats from Southern Gutaland in Sweden and, no, they are not Vikings at all as you were thinking. They are traders. You have heard of Beowulf I hope?"

"No, should I have?" And I began to shiver in my still-wet uniform. "Can you warm me up please as I do not want a cold again if I can help it."

"No, not at this moment in time. But you have something in your saddlebags to keep you warm, have you not? Your survival blanket is in your bag."

"Oh yes, I had forgotten all about it." And with that, I pulled off the wet cloak and undid all the harness, saddle bags and saddle on Thunder Hoof, put the cloak back on and pulled out my bag to find it. After rummaging in the bag, I pulled out a very wrinkled silver survival blanket which I had not seen in days or weeks as the last time I had seen it was when I met Tam Lin. The Merlin took off the red cloak I had on my shoulders and I wrapped myself in the survival blanket and sat down on my saddle and shuddered in some discomfort.

Looking up, I saw the last of the cliffs go by and raised my head over the side to see a very dark sea stretching to the horizon with dark clouds to the west. As I sat down Ormson's men put all the oars in the sockets on the side of the boat and as one side heaved on their oars, I felt the ship turn around and she wallowed in the swell and a wave broke over the side, then the other side pulled on their oars and they all pulled together. And they all got into a stroke and away from the cliffs, the Raven sped out into deeper water and then she began to roll with the swell. Now I have been out with my dad fishing before in a boat but this was different and it was possibly the biggest boat I have been on with no motor at all on board. Up and down she rolled and I heard a hiss of water on the side of the bow as I was sitting at the front of the ship. I looked at Thunder Hoof who was still asleep but with her legs swaying with the roll, but I was getting dizzy with the movement and then felt seasick. Up I moved to the side of the boat and, yes, I was seasick for some time. Back down, I rolled myself in my blanket and red cloak and tried to sleep and after some time, I did.

* *
* *

When I came to, I found myself lying by Thunder Hoof who was nice and warm on my back and who had somehow managed to find a way to lie by me. She was snoring in her sleep. As I rolled out of my blanket and cloak, I looked up to see the mast was up and the red and green sail was at full tilt.

The Raven was riding the waves with ease and, feeling a lot better in myself, I dragged myself up to see an overcast cloudy, gloomy day with drizzle in the wind and I shuddered in the cold wind.

Then there was a cry of "*Land Ho*" and, looking over the bow of the ship, I could just see through the mist and rain a long craggy island and I thought the only island I know of is Lundy far to the west of the Bristol Channel.

"That's Lundy," I said to the Merlin who was sitting down in the bow with Ormson. Ormson looked up at me.

"*Lundy. Is that what the island is called? Nice name for it.*" He stood up and he began to shout to the helmsman to stay away from the rocks which was at the end of the island. Then he shouted to his men to pull down the mast and sail and out with the oars. His men jumped to his commands and within minutes, the sail was down and stored away and the oars were out and pulling away from the rocks.

It was then I could see in the middle of the ship that was cargo all covered up with boxes and barrels roped up and a small wooden box on top with a black raven inside who was squawking harshly, "*Feed me, feed me!*"

I turned to the Merlin. "Why have they got a raven in a box on top of all the cargo?" I asked him.

"*Hm, so if they find themselves out to sea without land in sight they would release the raven who would fly up and up until it sighted land and then it would fly in that direction. If not, it would land back on the ship.*"

"Oh, I see. So they would go to where the raven was flying to if it saw land."

"*Yes, very good. You are learning how to live in this time, at last, my girl.*"

"Oh no, thank you. I wish to go home before I can get used to this mad world. As it is I have lost days off school work and I do look forward to it and going back to school."

"*Well we are on our way, girl, but we will have to put in at Lundy Island as there is a storm coming up the channel so we will have to lie up for some time.*"

"Good as I will be glad to get off this boat as I do not like being out at sea. What if the hag girls come back for me, with the trolls still after me I do not feel safe at all."

"*Well do not go near any deep water for a bit until we reach Watchet on the North Somerset coast in four days' time.*"

"Where in Somerset? I've never been to Somerset as yet, is it nice?"

"*Yes. In time, it will be full of cows' cheese, cider and sheep and good food as I recall. Oh look, here we go.*"

As I looked at the oarsmen, one side lifted up their oars and the ship turned to the left and the oarsmen on the left side pulled on their oars with some strength to bring the ship about to avoid some big rocks at the end of the island and into calmer waters and I saw a long stone beach with some craggy cliffs set back from the beach. "*Pull hard, lads!*" cried Ormson. "*Put her up onto the beach.*"

"*Hold on to something,*" said the Merlin as the ship with some speed hit with a crunch of pebbles. I managed to hold onto a rope as the ship ran up the beach and some men leapt out with ropes to hold her fast. It woke up Thunder Hoof who got up with a big yawn.

"*Are we there yet?*"

"Come on, Hoof, over the side with you." And with one leap she was over the side onto the beach and began to kick her legs as horses do.

"*Right, over the side with you.*" And at that, the Merlin picked me up and dumped me over the side into three feet of cold seawater.

"You idiot man, I am all wet again!" I cried as I waded out up the beach and squelched water out from my school shoes and cursing crazed wizards I ran after Thunder Hoof who had run up to the top of the cliffs.

Now running over pebbles and rocks in flat school shoes was no fun and I slid on seaweed and wet pebbles till I got to a path which lead up the cliff only to see my pony eating grass on top. "Hey, Hoof, what are you eating?" I asked as I got to her. She just looked at me and did a nice roll in the grass with her legs in the air. "Come on, you crazy pony, let's go for a ride before that storm hits us." So I jumped onto her back, held on to the bridle and we rode up and down the length of Lundy and I jumped off her. "I suppose you want to sit up here all day eating grass?"

"*Yes, I will.*"

"Oh well, I will be down on the beach if you need me at all so goodbye." As I made my way down to the beach, I saw the ship on her side with the sail pulled to one side making some sort of tent. As I slid down the beach, I could see some good-looking crags in the cliffs where I could make a camp as I did not want to sleep by the sea at all, so I went to fetch my saddle bags and all my things and made my way up to the cliffs where after some time, I found a suitable overhang for the day. I gathered in some driftwood to make a fire and dry seaweed to make a bed and I pulled out my bag to see what I had left inside my survival pack. Ah, yes, my firelighters, only two left now, and candles, matches, one fork, penknife and my survival blanket and cloak which I now had on, some food I had from Goewin back at the hill fort but no water. Then it began to rain so I started to make my fire, which took some time as the wood was all damp but in time I had a good fire going. I looked up to see two men come to me.

"Can we have some of your fire, lady Valkyrie, as our wood will not light up at all?"

*"*Yes, of course, you can, but better still I will light it for you." And digging into my bag I pulled out my last firelighter and followed them back down the beach which was easy-peasy and I did not slide at all.

At the ship, I saw some of the men doing various assorted sundry tasks. Two were cleaning a pile of crabs which were in abundance and the rest were looking cold and damp sitting all around under the sail and carrying out other tasks. In the middle of the camp was some wood in a pile and with my match, I lit the firewood and knelt down to it until it was burning well. *"How did you do that?"* asked Ormson who was looking at me in wonder as were all his men.

"Ah, you see it is Asgardian magic from the Dwarfs and not for the man at this time," I said taking my clue from Merlin. "Hey, where is the Merlin anyway?"

"Oh, he has disappeared up onto the Island. Last time we saw him was not long after you rode that horse of yours."

"Oh well, never mind. I will find him somewhere later on today." So feeding some wood onto the fire I had it going well for the happy men who were watching me and began to clap their hands now they could have some hot food. Saying goodbye, I walked back up to the crag as the rain began to hammer down so I was happy to get out of it. Back under my crag, I was nice and dry with my fire to keep me warm so after a bit, I made up my bed out of seaweed now all dry and lay down to see if it was all nice and flat. I saw in the rain two men who were carrying a pot. As I stood up the men came under the crag and put the pot down and pulled down their hoods and I saw they were the two men who asked for the fire.

"Valkyrie, would you like some crab soup?"

"Oh yes please." And pulling out my survival pot and carefully pouring some into it, I thanked them for the food. As they left, I dug in my food bag to find some more food to put in the soup and the spoon. I had a good hot dinner for once and I put out my pots to wash in the rain. I heard the crunch of pebbles and out of the rain came the Merlin looking very dry.

"Here you are. I have been looking for you. Can you help me find something I lost somewhere as it is not on the island anymore."

"Well, yes, but can it not wait until the rain has stopped?" I asked him.

"No, I need to find it now, so come on."

"Oh all right." And I began to put on my cloak.

"You do not need it," said the Merlin holding out his robe for me. *"You will be very dry under here."*

"All right." And I dropped my cloak onto my bed of seaweed. "Where are we going to now?"

"You will see, so under you get." And with that, I ducked under his robe to find it was not wet at all but warm and dry.

We made our way up to the top of the island but he turned to the left and as I had not been this way as yet; I asked him where we were going as there was only the end of the island.

"You will see but look down there." We were by some high craggy cliffs and I looked at a cove through the mist and rain. *"A big battleship will ram itself into this cove in the 1920s as they got lost in the fog on the way to the Isles of Scilly,"* said the Merlin, *"and no lives were lost. But come over here, girl, can you see what I can see?"* In the mist, I could make out some standing stones, two of them on the side of the cliffs all inscribed with weird-looking marks similar to the ones I had seen outside a church at Lewannick weeks ago. *"There, do you see,"* said the Merlin pointing down to some old worn stone steps leading down to the sea.

"I am getting a bad feeling about this," I said to him.

Chapter 16

Day 24 – The 13th Treasure

"Would you go down and see if you can see if there is a cave or something similar? You have to go under as well."

"Whoa! Not on your nelly!" I cried. "I am not going to go into that cold water for you or anybody again."

"Girl, if you want to go home you will have to. There is something I need you to get so we can pass through the shimmering divide unknown so stop your whinging and get down those steps and see what you can see. You had better have these goggles as well as it may be concealed and out of sight." And he handed them to me.

"But I have just got this uniform dry," I said, "and warm again. Can I not remove it, please?"

"No, you cannot. The spell is still on it as you well know. But I can put one more spell on it if you want to keep you warm under the water."

As I looked at the big cold waves I said, "Say it if you could, it looks cold to me." And with that, he hit me with his staff and said some words onto the top of my blazer and I felt warm all over my body from my head down to my toes. "Wow!"

"Now put the goggles on and tell me what you can see, girl."

Looking down at my feet, I could see the steps leading down into the sea for some distance down to a path which led to some sort of building under the sea some way out. I took off the goggles. "There is some sort of building down there," I said to him.

"Ah good. Does it look like a Corinthian temple, my girl?"

"What do you mean, Corinthian? With lots of columns and a big sloping roof?"

"Yes. Good, it will be inside so off you go, girl, now and be careful. There may be a guardian down there as well, which I put there some time ago."

"What do you mean, a guardian?" I said narrowing my eyes at him.

"Oh, just two guards to keep it hidden, but they must be dead by now."

"You think they will be dead by now? That is not good enough. I have been hunted by trolls, sea hags and by the Duke's men so what's next on the list?" I shouted at him.

"Girl, I cannot remember who or what I put down in the temple so please go and have a look."

"Gods, you will be the death of me yet," I said walking down the steps as I put back on the goggles. I stopped at the water's edge and looked into the depths. Oh well, here I go again and I stepped into the sea and as I did a big wave hit me in the face before I could take a breath. I expected to be dashed against the rocks any moment as the wave hit me, but no – my feet stayed on the stairway and to my relief, I was not forced back at all. As the wave receded, leaving me all drenched again, I looked down at my shoes to see they were fixed to the stairway, *so weird,* so I took some deep breaths and proceeded down the steps into the depths.

As the waters closed over my head, I was glad to see my school skirt was not flowing all around me as the gold rods were keeping it around my knees. Only my tie and hair were as my hands were holding down my blazer bottom so I could see where to go due to the Merlin's goggles and I did not need my dagger. Down, down, pushing my way past seaweed which grew on the sides but not the stairway itself at all. I could see this big building clearly through the seaweed blowing in the current. Then the steps levelled out and – still holding my breath somehow – I could see a long causeway in front of me disappearing into the blue waters.

As I stepped onto the causeway, my feet suddenly let go and I had to start to swim for it and around me, small shoals of fish swam all around crying, *"Hide, hide!"* I made my way to the temple to look for this treasure of Merlin's. It is most strange forever since I had to swim at St Nectan's pool I have had no fear of going underwater at all and it made no difference at all to swim in my poor old school uniform with all the gold rods keeping me down. Eventually, I made it to the building. It had some big stone steps going up into some vast antechamber with columns all around it and inside was all light and as my shoes hit the steps, I could stand upright. So I began to look at this marvellous temple under the sea. It was clear of seaweed and of white stone with ten or more steps, all clear as well.

With no fear of drowning, I walked up to the temple to have a look inside to see if Merlin's guardians were still there and, *wow,* saw one big sculpture of a warrior in what looked to me like scale armour with a spear and shield and helmet all lit up by light from somewhere. It was all in gold and a good twenty feet tall on its gold base and sitting in the middle of this big temple. I looked around and it was empty but for the sculpture. "What now," I said to myself as I stepped up to the sculpture for a better look at it and, *thud*, the shield suddenly dropped down to the base and the floor opened up under my feet and I plummeted down into darkness.

* *
* * * * * * * * * * * * * * * * * * * *

As I fell into the darkness, I thought I walked right into that one and no mistake but what was very strange was I was not in the water at all but in cold air. Then I hit the water feet first and my school skirt hit my nose with a thud as it flew up. Down, down I fell until I was immersed in lots of seaweed which stopped my fall somewhat till it began to wrap around my legs and arms until I was covered all over in it. As I struggled to free myself, the seaweed began to move my body through the dark weeds at some speed until I was deposited onto some steps where my feet hit stone and my head broke through the water into darkness. As the seaweed let go of me, I was able to stand up and reach into my wet blazer and pulled out my dagger to see where I had ended up. I found myself up to my neck in water and as I shone my dagger about me, I was still holding my breath. When I opened my mouth, the rank smell of damp air and the rotten smell of decaying seaweed made me cough.

The light illuminated a large room with two more 8 feet tall sculptures of warriors on both walls but in the middle was an ugly green stone idol holding up a robe of some kind in its arms. "Ah ha!" I cried as I stepped out of the water. This must be it but as I did so the idol started to glow as did the two sculptures who began to move their arms with two swords attached. "Damn it!" I cried. "Bloody Merlin and his guardians. Now, what can I do?"

I edged back to the seaweed and as I looked the sculptures turned into living flesh and both were female in old-looking Greek armour who both raised their swords and began to walk towards me.

"Yikes!" I cried as I turned and dove into the seaweed to hide and as I did, the seaweed began to grab me but I was able to cut my way through the weeds as my dagger was glowing like mad and it cleaved through them as if they were butter. Kicking my legs, I swam down to the rocks to find somewhere to hide in this green mass of seaweed root. As there was also a fast underwater current down there, I had to hold on to some of the roots as I had done when I swam out of the sea hag's cave. I put my dagger back into my blazer so as not to give my position away and sat on the bottom to see what would happen if I just sat still as I knew that the air spirit inside me would not let me drown as I held my breath.

Then off to my left side, I saw the weeds were being cut and beginning to rise and flow up and I knew it was time to go so I pushed off with my shoes and ascended up through the seaweed and swam to the stone steps where I was glad to see the guardians were possibly at the bottom looking for me so with that, I waded out and up to the idol with the robe in its arms. As I picked the robe out of its arms, the room lit up and started to glow red and began to screech. *Oh my goodness, is there a burglar alarm as well?* I looked around but there was nowhere to hide but back into the seaweed which was not a good idea.

As I spun around, I looked up and as I still had Merlin's goggles on, I saw in the roof of this underground water room a trap door on the top right above the idol so I hooked up my heavy wet skirt and climbed up the idol. On top, I had to stuff the robe into my blazer so as to free my arms and getting my balance, I reached up to find a lever which I pulled and I had to jump off as a ladder of some kind fell down along with lots of water. Picking myself up, I saw a gap in the roof and as the water had stopped up the ladder I climbed only to see the two sculptures come out of the seaweed pool. So I climbed up into a dark hole and on top of the ladder was one more lever which I pulled and was hit by heavy salt water in the face. I had to hang onto the ladder like grim death till I was able to climb out where I found myself under the big sculpture of the warrior.

As I looked down the hole I had just come out of, I could see movement below. *Oh God, they were still after me*, so I began to swim out of the temple and did not stop till I hit the steps and run up out of the sea. As I looked back under the water, I could see the two sculptures were on my tail and not very far away.

Out, out, I splashed and ran up the steps to the Merlin who jumped up at once when he saw my face. "Quick your bloody guards are on the way up!" I shouted at him as I made it to the top of the steps dripping water out of my uniform.

"*What!*" he cried, "*They are still alive? This cannot be.*" He looked down at the sea only to see two heads come up out of the sea and begin to come up the steps.

Chapter 17

Days 24 and 25 – All at Sea

"Quick, back to the boat!" he cried as he began to run to the path we had come up and I ran with him. I began to shout for Thunder Hoof who was still eating but she looked up at me with some worry in her eyes.

"Come on!" I cried. "We are getting off this island now." I ran to her and tried to slip onto her back but due to the wet skirt of my uniform, I fell off into a heap on the ground.

"Come on and stop mucking about!" cried the Merlin as he picked me up and sat me onto her back and I held on to her mane as she made her way down to the boat. Halfway down, I suddenly remembered my bag and cloak so slipped off her back and ran over to my camp and gathered all my things and ran down to the boat where all the men were in a hurly burly to get the boat out to sea.

With the Merlin shouting at the men to get the boat out to sea, I cried out to Thunder Hoof, "Get on board now!" I ran up and flung my things into the back of the boat and as I turned, I saw her leap onto the deck of the boat.

"Good pony!" I cried as I waded into the sea to help the men pushing the boat out and I put my hands on the stern of the boat as I could see the men struggle to get her afloat and with my arm ring of strength, I pushed as if the very life of me depended on it, which it probably did. And I did one big almighty shove and the boat slid over the pebbles and re-floated to a big cry from the men who all climbed aboard and as I tried to climb up my wet hands slid off the stern and I was face down in the sea.

"Pah!" I spat out seawater, which was now up to my waist.

There was a shout from the stern, *"Come on, girl, they're right behind you."* As I looked back, I saw the two guards were only ten feet away from me so all I could do was dive in the waves and swim under as it was no effort at all. It was so much easier to swim under the waves than on top. I had to do the crawl stroke and I was glad I had done up my blazer this time so it was no hindrance at all to swim in. Due to Mab's essence, I was soon alongside the boat. As I broke the surface, there was a shout and I looked up to see it was one of the men who had pulled me up the first time around and he lowered a rope to me with a loop at the bottom which I put my foot in and I was hoisted up in the hemp rope and over the side of the boat. *"You left it almost a little too late, my girl,"* said the Merlin. *"they almost had you."*

I was held up by the fair-haired man. *"Well done, my little Valkyrie, you pushed us off just in time from the cursed Hel things."*

As I stood dripping water all over the deck the Merlin looked at me. *"Have you got it then, my girl?"* And held out his hand.

"What? Oh, you mean this." And I reached inside my wet blazer and pulled out the robe and handed it to him.

"Aghh! It is all wet!" he cried. *"You could have kept it dry you know."*

142

"How?" I cried. "It was underwater at the time and I was being chased by your bloody guards so I had no time to keep it dry, so there." I wrapped myself up in my cloak and had a look at my pony.

Ormson then walked over to me and gave me a big hug. *"Well done, my young Valkyrie, you pushed us off in the nick of time with some strength, I see. I thank you also for the magic fire you made, my men were glad to have some hot food for once."*

"Oh, all I did was light the fire with my last fire stick, and I was glad to help. Mm, where are we going now?" I asked him.

"We are on the sea route to see my cousin who has set up a trading post on a bit of coast not far from some big hills where we trade for tin, pelts, lead and apple drink which is not to be found in my homeland."

"Ah yes, I know the word for that apple drink, it is called cider. My dad likes to drink it."

"Cider you call it. I will tell my cousin its name but come and sit with me and tell me of Asgard if you would. My men would like to hear what the gods are up to in Asgard." So I told him of my adventures in the bottom of the world ash tree and who I had met and how I had to find the Norn to stop her from taking girls from all the different realms to feed on their essence to try to keep herself young, and the bit where I was almost eaten by a troll witch who was in a small bottle but was killed by the goddess Artemis and I now had a blood price on my head as the crazy trolls think I killed her.

"Oh, gods, girl. I congratulate you on your enemies as we also have trolls in my homeland who hide in the hills and

valleys and only come out at night to hunt and steal and eat who they can catch."

"Ah yes, I have seen some Viking ships with dragon heads. I was told it is to scare away the trolls as they sail home." He gave me a mug of warm mead from one of his men who was the ship's cook. "Ah, yes, I have also seen the All Father, some otter god and the goddess of the dead, Hel and Queen Mab as well so you can tell I have been very busy of late."

He looked at me in shock. *"You, you know the Lady of the Dead? You have been to Hel and back. Gods the Valkyries put you through some hard tasks to be sure, do they not?"*

I just smiled. "Well, yes, it is a hard job to be sure." And I drank my mead, which warmed me up no end as I was still a bit cold from my swimming but the warm spell the Merlin had put on it was still working so my uniform was dry at last.

As he went off to see to his boat, I went to find my comb and I sat and combed out my long hair next to Thunder Hoof who was asleep again. I looked about me only to see the Merlin holding out the robe I had got for him to dry in the strengthening wind which was blowing the Sea Raven along at a good rate. I looked back to the island, which had disappeared and vanished into mist and a cloudy dark sky. Being too tired to stay up, I rolled myself up in my cloak and went to sleep next to Hoof.

It was the rain on my head which woke me up sometime later on as I pushed my way out of a pile of cloaks and oilskins, which were all brown in colour and all covered in fur. I looked up to see dark clouds and lots of rain in the air and a murky day.

"Good morning, young Valkyrie," said one of the men who were at the tiller or the rudder, who was holding on with some difficulty as the sea was quite rough and as I looked over the side I had a big faceful of sea water which woke me up no end.

"Haha, that will teach you to look over the side in a storm, my girl," said the Merlin who was sitting down by Hoof who had her legs braced again the pitch and roll of the boat. *"Come here, girl, and sit by me now and out of this rain."* As he was in a halo of dry air in the stern, I was grateful to be out of the rain for once. As we sat in silence, I looked at Hoof, who was still asleep with her head down with my blue cloak on her back. God, that horse can sleep anywhere.

"Merlin, can I ask you something? I was wondering why did Goewin and Brys have no tongues when I first met them as it was most strange to me as four days later on they could speak to me."

"Ah well, you see they had no tongues for a year because of the teaching as they had to use their minds to talk to one another. They are twins who know it is part of their teaching to be wizards."

"Oh, I see. But the hut, what is happening now as we left it at the hill fort? Do we have to rough it then with no hut or tent?"

"What, haha. Girl, am I not a wizard? We do not rough it at all when we get to Watchet, we can go to the hills where I know of a good inn on top and then we can hire a boat to get to Glastonbury so I can send you home."

"Oh good. I cannot wait to get this tie off and this uniform and into something more comfortable when I get home and have a hot shower and some TV and my bed. Oh yes, it will be good. Oh, I just remembered my bed fell down into that hole with all the other furniture in my room. What am I going to tell my mother? She will be furious with me."

"Do not worry too much as I would suggest the bedroom floor would be back up by now, but do not forget it has not happened yet, my girl, so if I remember I will be in Swansea at the time you fall down the hole."

"Do you mean you can be in the year 1970? Why did you not warn me at the time?"

"You, as I just said it has not happened yet so I did not know you back in the 1970s, but I do now so I will leave me some way in this time to tell me to go to your home. What was the date you fell down the rabbit hole?"

"Hey, can you not stop me from falling down in the first place? It would help."

"No, how can I as we have just talked about it haven't we, girl? But I will do something in your time to ease your mother as you are in this time now and as you are here, you have altered some things which will happen with you in this timeline as you have altered the future and past of all you have met, my girl."

"What do you mean? Just because I thought of Excalibur instead of my home I have changed events in this timeline so you say. It was not my fault I fell down that horrible hole into that water world and then into this one was it now? It was the Norn's fault I ended up here in the first place."

"Ah, so you say but you should have died at the well and not have come here in the first place to quote you."

"What? You bloody thing." And I jumped up and ran away from him and began to cry as I made my way to the bow of the boat to where Ormson was standing and he opened up his arms to me as I ran to him.

"What's up, my little Valkyrie? What is the matter with you? Has the wizard upset you?" he asked as he gave me a hug and I sobbed out my heart to him as I buried my face into his chest. *"Now then, my girl, do not be too upset. I will have words with the wizard for you so sit down on this bench with me in the warm."* And he covered me in his red cloak and I put my cold hands into my blazer pockets.

"Can I ask you a question, please? How did you know how to spell out my school motto as it is in Latin?" I asked, while drying my eyes on the end of his cloak.

"Oh, that was easy. My mother went to Ronum when she was young. It was she who taught me how to read Latin and all about Christendom and the angels and all the classical works she had seen and she was baptised as well. So you see that is how I could read it on what the wizard called a blazer."

"Oh, so you are a Christian then?"

"No, my father who follows the old ways still is a follower of Odin and Thor, Odin's son, and every ninth year he would go to Uppsala to the temple and the festival to the other gods." And he pulled out of his tunic a small hammer on a chain.

"So you are still a pagan then as I recognise that hammer." And I pulled the small hammer the slave girl gave me some time ago and I gave it to him as it was still in my blazer pocket.

"A goodly gift given, my Valkyrie. I will always treasure it. Oh, by the way, how is it you can speak my language as I have heard you have spoken with the wizard in some strange language. What is it as the lads were intrigued by it and how you can speak to the pony as well."

147

"Right, hmm, that would be the All Father's gift to me as he gave me a rune of wisdom to understand all that was said to me in this world and the speech of all animals, birds, fish but not reptiles which was the gift from Queen Mab."

"You have seen the All Father and been blessed by him," and he jumped up and shouted, *"lads, we have on my boat a true Valkyrie who has seen Odin and the Lord Thor Odinson."* And then he held up the hammer I had given him and it was shining bright in his hand and all his men gave a great shout of joy to see it and to make matters worse there was a big clap of thunder overhead and a stroke of lightning flashed in an arc over the boat and all the men jumped and began to wave whatever weapons they had at the time in their hands. But one man overdid it and jumped onto his oar bench yelling the name Thor and with a yell fell overboard into the sea, and before I knew it my life-saving teaching came back to me and I was up and over the side of the boat and diving into the sea.

* *
* * * * * * * * * * * * * * * * * *

And into the horrible cold brackish brown seawater, I dove and I could not see a thing till I came up some way from the boat and saw the man with his hands in the air. "Hold on!" I yelled to him as I swam to him so grateful for Queen Mab's essence in me as I got to him in no time at all and gripped his ankle and pulled him to me and thrush his arms apart as he tried to grab my arms and turned him onto his back. "Do not struggle and we will both be safe." And I pulled him back to the boat, which was already on the turn to pick us up. As she came about, the oarsmen were working like mad and I redoubled my efforts as the man was fully clothed in a wool cloak and boots, making it hard to pull him. Then the boat came alongside and a rope was thrown to us and I pushed the man up first as he grasped the rope and was pulled up and as I let go, I was sucked under by the passage of the boat right under the keel and to my horror there was one of the hag's girls who was clinging to the bottom of the boat with her claws.

I must have done an underwater screech as she looked at me and unhooked her claws which gave me time to pull the dagger out of my pocket and as she opened her mouth to scream at me, I dove down out of the way of her stoic wave and out of fear I swam down into darkness. *Damn things,* I thought as I sank down. It must have been at the island looking for me all this time and I shuddered at the persistent efforts of the trolls to get me in their claws. Right, time to make some distance from the sea hag girl and I thrust my arms through the water in the hope that she would not see as I swam up to the surface and as my head broke the top it was only to see the boat had moved on some way into the mist. "Hey, hey!" I shouted as I fought for buoyancy with my arms in the air but as I was going up and down in the surf it was doubtful anybody could see me through the drizzle. So I began to swim after the boat and into the crawl stroke which was so difficult to do because of the waves in my face and as I was about to dive down there was a powerful tug on my right foot and I was tugged under the surface.

* *
* * * * * * * * * * * * * * * * * *

And down, down I was pulled into the depths and I could not see as my school skirt was up to my face hitting my nose which was painful due to the gold rods. Then I was in clear water and I saw the hag girl as I, at last, pushed my sodden skirt down. She let go of my ankle and spun me around to face her as she gripped my sleeve with her right claw and tried to rake me with her left one which I dodged just in time. I grabbed her arm with my right hand and forced her arm back to her face. Then she fought to free herself from my grip and my dagger was in her face blinding her eyes and with a big tug, she tore herself free and let go of my arm and shot off into the dark.

"On no, you don't!" I cried, bubbles flowing out of my mouth. "You come back here." And I kicked my legs into motion and thrust my body through the water after her, so grateful once again for Mab's essence in me as my full school uniform was no hindrance to me now and for Merlin's spell of warmth as I would have been dead of hypothermia by now in the cold sea. With my dagger of light, I could see her legs to into some weeds on the sea bed to try to conceal herself in them and as I got to the weeds she was gone. Then I saw a blur of movement someway off and for some time we played cat and mouse in the murky seaweed beds. At last, I managed to corner her by some rocks and I got a good look at her and, oh my she was all covered in scars and wounds on her body and half her fins were missing and she shouted some gibberish at me as I thrust the dagger into her mouth whereupon she screamed and went into some sort of seizure and she began to expand. I pulled my dagger out and quickly swam back and then she exploded into a green mass and was simply gone with some speckles of light.

The exploding force drove me back into the seaweed beds where I lay for some time as I was somewhat exhausted by my swimming down after her and I hoped the other one was nowhere nearby and then I was attacked by a big red lobster. "Get off you!" I cried as I pushed it away and rose off the bottom up to the surface. Up, up I swam till my head hit the top where I spat out the seawater in me and as I shook the water out of my eyes I could see a boat not far off with a man inside with a fish net in his hands.

Good, now I can ask him for some directions to Watchet, I hoped and I did the crawl stoke over to this boat, but as I got near I cried out to him, "Hello, hello!" And I splashed the seawater with my hands. He looked up in shock to see me swimming to his boat and he sat down and pulled out a big club and he held it up. "Whoa, whoa!" I cried. "I will not harm you." I lost my grasp on the side of his boat which rose up and down with the swell of the sea.

"What do you want with me?" he cried. He swung the club at me, which I had to dive under the water to avoid.

As I came back up I said, "All I want is to ask you the way to Watchet, please." And I pulled away from his boat. And with a trembling arm, he pointed to the right. "Thank you," I said to him as I dived down under as it was more effort to swim on top of the sea and back under I began to swim in the direction he has shown me. I had to come up now and then to see if I was going the right way when I saw through the sea fog a big hill all clad in dark trees and I heard the sound of the tide on the seashore.

At last, I thrashed my way through the sea until I saw the beach of grey stones then the sea picked me up and pushed me up onto the shore where at last I could stand up, my clothes literarily dripping with seawater, and I had to shake myself all over like a dog to get dry. After a bit I had to sit down on a rock to catch my breath, swimming is good for your health they say but I had done enough in the last two weeks to last me a lifetime. I tried to ring out some water from my skirt and undid my blazer and patted my belly. I must have lost some weight with all this swimming I had done in the last week or so.

So up I got and ran up this beach to get some warmth into me and it was good to run as I had ridden for some time in the queer world I had found myself in. As I ran, I saw some people by a small river with pots and pans in the water. As I got to it I could see beautiful clear water and I sank down to my knees and cupped my hands to drink my fill to get the taste of seawater out of my mouth and wash my face and hands also my salt-covered hair as best as I could. Pity the river was too shallow to go in to wash myself all over.

So up I splashed across this river and ran up the beach stopping sometimes to have a rest but as I ran on the beach began to get too stony for me to run any further so I was forced to go up onto land where the running was hard so I had to walk it. As it was getting on to night time the setting sun shed light onto a long ridge of hills stretching inland and all dark, and then I heard the sound of thunder in the distance and looked up to see no thunder clouds overhead so it can only be one thing so I ran to the only high bit I could find and began to wave my arms in the air.

And out of the gathering dark rode my pony who was shouting my name and joyfully I ran to meet her with tears in my eyes at this happy meeting and I clung to her as she ran to me.

Chapter 18

Days 25 and 26 – Hills

"My pony!" I cried as she almost ran me over in her haste to get to me and we danced around one another in a joyful reunion.

"How did you get here, how did you know how to find me?" I cried to her with tears running down my face.

"They said you would be dead by now but I knew you could survive in water for some time due to Mab's essence in you, my girl."

"Ah, and you knew how to find me by going down the coast until you found me, my good girl, and where is the Merlin? Did he send you to find me?"

"No, I did it on my own. When the boat got to the port, I jumped overboard into the sea."

"What you swam in the sea, you mad pony, but I thank you for it so let's go back to the boat and see what is happening." I jumped onto her and I rode bareback all the way to the boat Thunder Hoofing as she ran.

So we rode on until it got too dark to see so I dismounted and led her on until I could smell wood smoke from a nearby hill on my left and we pushed past some trees and I saw a glimmer of light all the way around a wall of wood and some men stood by some doors who shouted, *"Hey you, come here to me."* As they run up to me, I recognise the man I had to pull out of the sea some time ago and he had a torch in his hand. *"Hold, look, Sven, it's the Valkyrie who pulled you out of the sea. She is not dead at all."* And as one they lowered their shields and threaded their spears through the armholes to make a platform and told me to get on. *"Come, Lady Valkyrie, we will see you to the hall where Ormson will be glad to see you no end as he thinks he had lost you to Hel."*

"Haha." I laughed as I stepped up onto the shields. "I have already been there, lads, it is not nice at all." As I held on to their two helmets, they lifted me up into the air and off I go up to the doors as now I recognise this as a small hill fort. Inside, I saw a long hut with some small outhouses all around. As I look back to Thunder Hoof, I see her run into one. "Ah, I bet that is the stables. Good Girl." We got to a door and as one they hit the door with a bang three times then three more and three more. Then the door was flung wide open and stood in the doorway was Ormson with a look of wonder at me.

"My Valkyrie!" he cried. *"You—you are here and not in Hel at all, come in, come in."* And with that, he picked me up by my arms and held me till I was on the ground.

Inside, a score of men and women sat at a table with a fire down the middle and a top table at the front end with a man in good-looking clothes who was sat down but stood up as we came in. *"Listen good people of this port and my good company. Here is Angelina of Asgard the young Valkyrie who jumped into the sea after Sven who fell overboard and pulled him to me who I then saw was pulled under my ship not to be seen again and now here she is!"* cried Ormson as he held up my arm for all to see. *"Come to the top table, Valkyrie, and tell us all of your time at sea, if you would,"* asked Ormson as he walked me up through the hall and all the people looked at me in some wonder.

"I need to sit by the fire first if I can," I told him, "as I am still a little wet and damp from my swim in the sea." And I sat down.

"Yes, my Valkyrie, and I have had words with the wizard for you as he said some bad words to you, did he not?"

"Mmm, yes he did," I said, holding my hands out to warm them, wishing I could take off my school shoes to warm my feet. Just then, I was given a bowl of food and a wooden cup of mead, which I drank down at once. "Ahh, this is better." Asking for more as I ate my food and suddenly feeling hungry for the first time since my food at the island a day ago and with all that swimming I had to do with the sea hag's girl as well, no wonder I was so hungry. After two more bowls of food and drink, I was feeling much better in myself.

"Now I will tell you all of what happened to me when I pulled Sven out of the sea," I said as I sat at the top table now nice and dry for once with hot food inside me. "My Lord Ormson, did you know that a sea hag was under your boat all the time looking for me as she had tried to kill me once before," I said as I hammered it up to them all. "Yes, as I was pulled under the boat, she was clinging to the bottom of your boat and I had to fight her to the death through all the underwater seaweed beds and for hours. We hunted in and out until I killed her with my dagger." And I pulled out my dagger, which lit up the hall to lots of shouts and screams as the light was so bright to them all due to the darkness of the hall.

"Oh, so sorry," I said as I put it back inside my blazer, "that dagger will keep absorbing the life force of all it hits, it is one of the things it picked up from that sword Excalibur or Caledfwich, which means cut steel so sorry again." As I was about to sit down next to the old man in the good clothes and I bowed to him. "Thank you for having me in your hall this night, my Lord Grendel Bane."

"Ah ha, you give me great honour, young Valkyrie. You have been talking to my nephew Ormson of my tall tales of when I was the sword bearer to my king Beowulf when he had to slay the Hel monster Grendel and his mother the water-troll." I shuddered at the name of the water troll remembering the time when one almost ate me. *"Oh you look so sad, young Valkyrie, what is it I said to you?"*

"Oh, it was the time when I let out of a bottle and a witch troll who was seeing me through the roots of Yggdrasil, the world ash tree to the Norns, tried to eat me up."

His eyes went wide. *"You met a troll mother and what happened to her?"* he asked.

"I was rescued by my goddess who killed the troll. Now the bloody trolls want my head and I had to kill a sea hag which they sent to kill me and take my head to them."

"By the gods, you have had some good adventures, young one. Here, have some more mead in you." And he gave me one more cup of mead.

* *
* * * * * * * * * * * * * * * * * *

And you can tell by all the mead I had drunk and hot food in me, I awoke under the table in the morning with a thick head and all around me were the bellies of the people who were still asleep in the dark hall. I pulled myself up and moved outside to a dry day and found a water butt and stuck my head in.

Ah, better. As I shook out water from my hair and eyes, the bright sunlight hurt my eyes as it was still early in the morning with a blue sky to the east and no clouds overhead. Oh good, the storm had passed over for which I was glad as I was sick of the rain on my head. And then out of one of the huts Hoof ran over to me so I gave her a hug and some pats. "Oh come, girl, you need a brush down so let's go and find my bag shall we?" And I hopped onto her back and rode her out through the gates which were open and down to the port which was no more than some big huts in a circle with a fence around it and over to a small river.

Out in the sea was the boat on its side with some men who were unloading the goods. As I rode up, I could see the two men who pulled me out of the sea who were seeing to the unloading by the local men who stopped what they were doing and all looked at me. *"Good morning to you, young Valkyrie. You swam out of the sea I see, Ormson was most put out by you diving into the sea to help Sven out and then you did not come back up. We were sure you had sunk to the bottom, but the wizard said you could live under the water as well as on land so not to worry too much."*

"Yes, I can, and under your boat was a sea hag which was looking for me and I had to battle her under the sea and then I had to kill her. You and your boat had gone when I came back up, so I swam to the shore. Where is the wizard this morning?" I asked as I got off Hoof.

"Look over there." And one of the men pointed his finger to one of the huts and as I turned around, I could see the Merlin was sitting down by one of the huts with his hood over his head with all my stuff in a pile by him.

As I walked up to him he looked up at me. *"Ah, I see you are back, my girl. Did you have a nice swim in that cold sea then? It was very brave of you to dive in to save that man. Ormson was in a fit when you did not come up and I had to tell him that you could live under the water for some time. So, tell me what happened down under the sea."*

"Hmm, what do you care if I live or die? I just want to go home. You promised to send me back to my timeline so please can we get going?"

"Oh, all right, and I must apologise to you for saying some bad words to you. Can you forgive me? It was not nice and in the heat of the moment."

"Good. I am glad that is straightened out." And I began to put all my things onto Thunder Hoof's back. On with my boots, cloak and hood as it was very cold out on this February morning.

"Can you now keep on all the clothes, girl? As you have to be seen as one of the Priestesses of Avalon so we can travel with no hindrance to Avalon."

"Do I have to keep my head down all the way?" I asked him.

"Yes if you can. It would help me to keep it up as a prospect of me taking you to Ynys-Witrin, the Isle of Glass as the locals call it."

"Oh, okay, I will," I said as I got on my pony and tucked in my skirt under the saddle and spread my coat out over

Hoof's back and pulled up my hood over my head and looked at him.

"*Right, off we go. Follow me.*" And he began to move off to the distant hills following up the beach till we got to the foot of the hills. "*Right, up we go. You will like these hills. They are called the Quantock Hills in time. Very nice on a good day as you can see for miles all around. You had better get off and walk it up as it can be a very steep slope.*" So I had to get off and climb up holding on to Hoof as she made light work of it. As we got to the top, he turned to me and held out his arm. "*Look you can see the Somerset levels from here.*"

As the day was now nice and clear and the storm had passed over in the night, I had a clear view of the Severn estuary and over the hill to my left were some big brown hills where I had come ashore and down into Watchet. But as I turned to my right, I was beholding a view of a vast lake stretching to some hills all the way into the distance with some large island there and there were lots of big trees. But to my joy, there was the Tor of Glastonbury some way off in the distance.

"That is Glastonbury Tor but why is there no tower on top?" I asked him for I had seen it many times in pictures.

"*There will be a tower on top but not until 1450 AD, people will use it for many things to come right up to the civil wars as I have seen gun slits in on its side. So get on your pony and let us go all the way into Somerset until we hit the water then we will see you on your way home, my girl.*"

Chapter 19

Days 26 to 28 – Water, Water Everywhere

So we travelled all day on top of the hills that he called the Quantocks, passing lots of cairns and Bronze Age barrows all around on this good track. He said we had to follow and all I could see were lots of heathers and stumped trees with deep valleys but not a soul to be seen at all. And the wind was very gusty on top. It made it hard to keep my cloak down at all so in dismay, I got off Hoof and led her by hand till we came to what he said was Thorncombe Hill where we stopped for a rest and where he pulled out of his robe a bag. He prepared out of it a good breakfast and as all this fresh air had made me so hungry I set to as did Hoof as well, nibbling at the heather. *"See we wizards do not rough it at all, so eat up, girl, we still have a long way to go today."*

As I sat on my cloak, I could see a big barrow and I asked him who put all these barrows there. *"The ancient ones, my girl, long before the Romans came to this land and even the Celts, your people, turn up in this land, my girl."*

"So how old are they then?" I asked.

"Oh, at least 3,000 years old, Neolithic and early Bronze Age I would think. If you have finished, let's go on." So up the track, we carried on our way till we got to some plush place

161

called Triscombe Stone where we find what he called an inn which was no more than a hut next to a stumped stone where he said we were to spend the night.

"What is in there?" I said. "Is it big enough to get into?" I asked looking at it, doubtful as to its appearance.

"Yes, it will do. Now go and stable the pony at the back and keep your head down."

"All right," I said and I pulled her, "come on, Hoof, let's see what's on offer." And as I round the hut to my unlooked-for relief was a good-looking stable for six horses with water and grain and lots of hay.

"Nice."

"What, yes come on in." And I undid all the tack of her then fed her and gave her a good rub down and looked at her hooves which were still in good shape. I gave her some water and said good night as I shut the stable door. As I went to pick up my saddle with the bags around the hut came the Merlin.

"Ah, here you are. The supper is ready, come on, girl."

"Good. What is it?" I asked him as I walked with him to the hut's door.

"It is mystery meat pie tonight so do not look too close."

"Oh, great," I said as he opened the door.

"Put the saddle on that pole over there but bring your bags with you." And he walked down some steps into what can only be an underground room with warmth coming up from all the candles I could see at the bottom. As I walked down into this room, I saw lots of candles on the walls and a big fire hearth with a woman chopping up some meat. All around were some round tables with stools. *"Keep your head down, girl, and do not talk to anybody at all."*

162

"Okay," I muttered as I sat down next to him and as the old woman came over to us, I lowered my head when she got near me. She then bowed her head to me. I looked at the Merlin as if to say, *what do I do now*? as she was still in a bow.

"*Say thank you, girl,*" he muttered to me.

"Thank you," I muttered in a low voice.

Then she stood up and said, "*I thank you, Priestess of Avalon. I bid you welcome to my humble inn. I hope you will be happy here tonight.*"

"Yes, thank you." She put out some bowls and cups all made out of wood and then she moved over to the fire hearth to put her pot over the fire.

"*Well done, girl. Keep that up and we will have no trouble when we get to Glastonbury. Oh, here comes the food.*" And the old woman began to lay out the hot food into the bowls.

I looked up at the Merlin. "What do we eat it with?" I asked him.

"*You have that Roman spoon I put in your bag do you not, my girl?*" As I dug into my bag and after some time, I found it at the very bottom of the bag.

I looked at him. "Did you loot this off the Duke then?" And he just smiled at me.

"*Eat your food, girl, before it gets cold.*"

* *
* * * * * * * * * * * * * * * * *

So, after a good night's sleep on the floor where I was nice and warm, I was given some hot water to wash my face and hands before we started off on our way to Avalon.

Outside was a gloomy day with rain in the air and cold so I was glad of my cloak and boots for once as I got Hoof out to put on the saddle. *"Girl, it may be the last day for me in this world, as I may not be able to go with you to Avalon."*

"What, but you must. I was given you by the gods to see me to Avalon."

"Yes, girl, but I will not be able to go on the small boat the mad wizard is going to see you to Avalon in, now can I, girl?"

"Oh, I had not thought of that. No, you could not as it would not be possible for you to get on a boat."

"So look out for a rainbow girl later on today." And in tears, I saddled her up, up came my bag and I got on. I worried all day as we moved all along the hills and as it was raining all day, I was very miserable and cold despite the warmth of my blazer and the warm pony I was sitting on and this gloomy day did not help one bit.

Not even a herd of deer I saw could lighten my mood. They ran off when they saw us and as the hills were getting lower as we trekked through these hills, the cold level was chilly and when we got to the lower track, we were in the mist, so I had to get off as the going was not too good. *"Girl, I see a hill where we can have some rest and some food!"* shouted the Merlin through the mist. *"Come on and stop your dawdling, girl, and pull that pony along."*

"Oh good," I muttered, water dripping off my nose as I followed him up a hill with one more big barrow on top and into the sunshine. It was then that Hoof stood very still and was looking up at the sky and she would not move at all despite my pulling her. Then she looked at me.

"My girl, I think this is goodbye as I have to go back to Asgard this day."

"What do you mean go? You were a gift to me."

"I know but this is the end, look." And as I looked up at what she was looking at only to see a rainbow appear high up in the sky and a horse rode all the way down it.

"Gods!" cried the Merlin. *"It is a Valkyrie come to take back your pony. Quick, girl, off with all your fare and the saddle and bridle as well."* And as she was a bit frisky it was hard work to do as she would not keep still at all. As we worked to unload her, I heard a song in the wind and it went like this:

Three times nine girl
But one rode ahead
White-skinned under her helmet
The horses were trembling
From their mane, dew fell into the deep valley and haze in the wood
Whoever sees me, good fortune comes to them there.

All that song was hateful to me. Finally, we managed to get it all off in time. Then Thunder Hoof ran up and down the hill in joy as me and the Merlin watched this figure ride down the rainbow on a big horse until this Valkyrie landed by us. As she slipped off the horse, I noticed there was no saddle at all and as she walked up to us she was all in something like strange armour of burnished scale, which reflected the light of the rainbow. In one hand, she held a long spear which shone light rays. She was very slim with long legs dressed all in fur, a tall, winged helmet and a blue dress with a red cloak.

"Hail to you, wizard, and to you, Angelina Troll Slayer. Your deeds are to this day sung in all the inns in Asgard and

through the nine realms. I give you a good welcome." And she bowed to us.

"Welcome, Valkyrie, to middle-earth. I take it you are here to take the pony back to Asgard as she cannot enter the water lands of this world as she would not go on any boat we find," said the Merlin to her. *"Girl, say goodbye to your pony as she has to go back to Asgard as the Valkyrie has to take her back this day. As you know, she cannot go with us anymore as we are to go by boat."* And in floods of tears, I ran to Thunder Hoof and gave her a big hug and a kiss all over as she licked me back.

"Ho, girl, I am going to miss you so much but do not be dismayed. I will see you again one day, the gods willing, so goodbye, my sweet girl. Do not trust that mad wizard at all, girl." And then she ran to the Valkyrie who by now was back on her horse and as she took hold of her mane and bowed to us once more and as one they all flew up into the rainbow and were gone.

"Ah well that want well them Valkyries can be a bit nasty sometimes to mere mortals. I am glad only one showed up and not nine of them. Oh, stop your crying, girl. You knew that was going to happen one day." And he gave me some clothes to blow my nose. *"Now then, what do we do with all your saddle bags and the saddle my girl?"*

"What?" I cried as I sat down on the saddle still in tears as to what had just happened as I had just lost my best friend in this horror of a world and why did she call me a troll slayer?

"Get up, girl, and stop that crying. By the gods, if I lost something of mine I would not cry over it, I would get a new one, so come on we have some way to go before it gets dark. I know why she called you troll slayer," he said as he pulled

me up. *"Get up."* And he pulled me up. *"You dig out your bag, girl. I am going to shrink the saddle and your saddlebags so small you can get them into your bag so when you get home they will grow back to normal size, and the boots as well."*

"You beast you. Now I have got to walk it. How far is it we have got to go?"

He looked at me. *"Beast, I? I have been called worse by better people, my girl, so stop your whingeing and get on with it now."* And he did something to the saddle with his staff.

* *
* * * * * * * * * * * * * * * * * *

And in ten or more minutes or so all was packed away and I had the unaccustomed feeling of my bag on my back after so long without it as the last time I had it on was in the Norns cave weeks ago. So off we trundled up this muddy track, my poor school shoes and socks all covered in cold wet mud. I was not happy at all, and then the Merlin looked back the way we had just come. *"I know where we are. This hill is called Merrdige Hill. I have been here before,"* he said as he looked at me, *"only three miles to go, girl, till we get to Fitzwarren Hill Fort, mind you, the Ordnance Survey maps still call it a settlement if I remember right, which is not the right word for it."*

"As if I care," I muttered as I tugged my hood down a bit more as the rain was running down my nose, "and try to keep out of the deep puddles."

"Girl, remember to keep your head down as you are meant to be a novice on her way to Yrns-Witrin and do not look at anybody as well." He turned off the track down to

some woods onto a small path full of wet ferns and weeds, and I wished I still had my long boots on but he had put them with the saddle and bags then he had shrunk it all, as this path was a slippery as the track we had just left. So down and down into this wood, he dragged me till we came to the bottom of the hills. *"Ah, Cothelstone,"* he said to me as he helped me over some wet logs. There was a small stone and wood hut of sandstone with some clean water flowing out of some stones. *"It is St Agnes's Well, girl. It is good for healing and wishing and if you are quiet, you can see Somerset Pixies as well."*

"Sod the bloody pixies I say," I said as I sat down on the only dry spot I could find and kicked off the mud of my shoes, my black socks plastered with it and so cold to touch as they were covered in it all the way up.

"Here, drink this." And he handed me a cup of water. *"It will make you feel better, my girl."*

"Huh," I muttered as I took a sip, *oh my God,* the taste was nice and I did not know how thirsty I was so I drank it all down and asked for more.

"See," he said as he gave me one more. *"Did I not say it would do you good, so drink up and let's get on. We have got to go over some fields and have a river to wade across yet."* He was not kidding. We walked down a long slope over lots of fields with wet furrows down to swampy bits. *"Girl, walk in my footsteps and do not wander off it at all,"* he said as he turned to me as we came to the end of the fields. And all I could see was water, water everywhere and he walked on all I could do was to walk behind him as we waded through this foot-high water. The only good thing about it was it washed off the mud from my legs and shoes.

"Right, girl, this is where it will be a lot deeper but you will be all right." And he hooked up his robes to reveal long walking boots up to his waist.

"Oh, I see you get the boots and I have to put up with wet feet." And I pulled up my cloak and waded after him. As it got deeper, I was up to my waist in cold river water, not nice, until the Merlin blew a hole through some bulrushes with fire from his staff which made all the seeds fly up in the air. *"Come girl, I can see the far bank."* And he made his way through the lot of them up onto the bank, where he held out the staff for me to grasp. He pulled me out. I had to wring out water from the skirt and squelched out cold water from my shoes and wrapped myself up in my cloak which I had kept dry at least.

"Look!" he cried, pointing to a hill not too far away up a slope. *"We can stay there tonight in good beds and hot food."* As I was now chilly and my feet and legs were so tender, I was looking forward to some warmth and a place to lay down for once. *"Right, not far now."* He took my arm and up this slope, we trudged, up until we hit a path which led up to the hill and yes I could see a small hill fort with some huts and people.

And for once, he was correct as we were fed and watered and were given a hut to sleep in, for which I was so grateful after all the walking I had done. I stayed in bed for most of the day as the Merlin was in talks with the headmen as to hire a boat to get to Glastonbury by way of the lake villages across the Somerset levels to Avalon.

Chapter 20

Days 28 to 29 – To Avalon

It was not until mid-afternoon that I got out of bed. I was so bored that I got dressed and sat on the only bit of furniture which was an old Roman chair with woodworm and I looked outside to see this hill fort was more farm than anything I had seen before as most of the hill was full of livestock.

As I looked out, I saw the Merlin come out of one of the round huts with one of the head men and some girls in tow and they all walked over to the hut I was in. So I got up and walked out of the hut to do my bit as a priestess of Avalon and pulled the cloak around my legs to hide my shoes and socks. As we had arrived here, it got dark I had not yet seen the headman and he was quite tall for a Celt and was in good clothes, as were the girls. *"Hail to you, priestess. We are humbled by your visit to us this day. We have not seen one of your kind in a long time. We are blessed by your timely appearance. If you would be so kind as to bestow good grace over this farm and help my girls to bless the spring crops if you would, priestess."* I bowed my head in reverence to his plea and had a pleasant two hours with his girls blessing the spring crops as I sang some songs to the soil to his girls' delight as they danced up and down the rows. And with gifts of food and water, we were taken down to some long jetty which reached out into the reeds where there were long boats perfect for journeys through the marsh and the reeds and with two men who would see us to Avalon. The two men had long poles which they used to push us off and at last, I was on my way to get home, *I hoped*, and then it began to rain again and I pulled my hood down a bit more.

"Ah, yes, the locals call this February Field dyke, girl," said the Merlin as he sat behind me. *"This is why Somerset is called Somerset as you can only come here in the summer, haha, as it is one big lake for most of the year."* And we came out of the reeds into the flow of a big lake which one of the men said was a river in the summer. As he poled up and out into the main flow, out of the reeds flew lots of birds, mainly water birds. This was a birdwatchers' paradise as there were hundreds and hundreds of them. We travelled all that day until it got dark when we came to what the Merlin said was a lake village where we had to spend the night. There were two families living there who put us up for the night in one of the huts as welcome guests. Supper was bottled fish with some kind of bird which was so delicious I asked what the bird was. The bird was a swan. Oh my, but it was too late now. I had just eaten one of the Queen's birds, but it was so nice.

Before I went to bed, three children asked me to sing to them, so in a low voice, I sang some rhymes and psalms to please them.

* *
* * * * * * * * * * * * * * * * * *

The next day was bright with blue skies as we set off waving goodbye. The two men pushed on through the reeds until the Merlin pointed to a small hill on my left side. "*Burrow Mump, that will be a hill fort one day in about five hundred years' time and Alfred the Great was up here hiding from the Danes in the eighth century.*"

"Good for him," I said as we pushed on. The reeds were now so high I could not see past them so to pass the time, I put my hand in the water to see how cold it was.

"*Do not put your hand in,*" cried one of the men at the back, "*there are leeches in the water in this bit of the marsh.*"

"What!" I cried as I pulled my hand out and looked for them. "*You be careful, girl. Leeches can leave some nasty blood inside you. You do not want to be bitten by one if you want to go home,*" said the Merlin and he had a good look at my hand.

Then we were in a big clearing surrounded by reeds and on my left side was a large island raised above the reeds. "Are we not going to stop here?" I asked the man who had just put his pole in the water.

"*No, priestess. We do not go to that island anymore as it is full of bad men and women and this clearing was not here last year.*" And he put the pole he was holding into the marsh water then something shot past my nose and landed in the water with a splash and as I looked at what it was there was a loud scream from the man in front of the boat as two arrows hit him in the front and he dropped the pole and clutched one of the arrows as he pitched overboard.

In some fright, I looked to my left to see four boats come out of the reeds with men with bows in front and with two men rowing at the back. I saw them begin to draw back on the bows as I reached forward to grasp the pole as it drifted past and pulled myself up. "Do something!" I cried to the wizard as I stood up and pushed down with the pole with all my strength as an arrow hit the top of the pole and my cloak was suddenly hit by one and the boat had been hit in between me and the Merlin.

"*I am on to it, girl!*" he cried as the man at the back was hit in the leg, he jumped into the water to his friend with a cry of pain.

"*Hold on!*" shouted the Merlin as he hit the boat with the staff which began to glow and the boat shot over the water so fast, I fell onto my back with the pole still in my hands and in no time at all, we were in the reeds to the cries of the men in the boats as we had left them far behind us.

"What was that?" I cried to the Merlin as I picked myself up only to find an arrow at the back of my cloak which I had sat on and began to shake in fear and trembling all over in fear as to what had just happened.

"*Keep your head down, girl. We are not out of the woods yet. There may be more hiding in the reeds. Oh, look, we have a hole in the boat.*" An arrow had gone right through the side of the boat.

"What do we do now? We have lost the two locals!" I cried as I pulled the arrow out of my cloak with trembling fingers to see a hole in the cloth. I broke the shaft and dropped it over the side and pocketed the arrowhead in my blazer as a keepsake as it almost had me.

"*We keep moving on, girl, until I see something I recognise, so keep down, girl, until we hit land.*"

As the boat ploughed its way into the reeds, I lay on my belly trying to see where we were going till I saw some high hills. "Look, land!" I cried to him.

"Where to?" he said as he turned to his right.

"There, look, land." And I pointed my arm in the air. "A high hill on your right-hand side." And as he pointed his staff to the right, the boat turned on its side almost tipping us over until I rolled to my left side and it carried on its way into the reeds upsetting waterfowl as we ploughed on.

"Ah yes," he cried. *"This is High Ham Hill. I know where we are, girl. We have to turn to the left. Hold on."* And as before, I rolled to my left as he moved his staff and we skirted by the hill and out into the open water and before us was a long ridge of hills. *"We keep on this way,"* he cried, *"until we hit a place called Compton Dundon as I have been this way before."*

I looked back to where we had just come from to see if we were being watched by the men in the boats, but to my relief, there was no sign of them. "Where are we going to?" I asked him and he pointed the staff at a high hill to the right.

"We will land on the left side of the hill, girl. I know of a path which goes to the top of that ridge and from there you will see your Avalon."

"You mean I am at Avalon already?" I cried.

"Oh good. How long till we get there?" I asked him.

"Not until night falls, girl. We will have to go the back way in as I cannot see the way to go in daylight. The rubics I put on your arm ring will grow red when we get to the sanctuary at Ynys Witrin. Now girl, get a hold of that pole. I am going to stop this boat, you can push us to the side of this hill so get up."

174

"All right." And I pulled the pole to me and stood up and put the pole into the dark water and pushed us along as the boat had by now slowed down.

"Here, make for that path of reeds over there, girl."

"What?" I dug in the pole to move the way he was pointing his staff and I punted on I could see a bank of long weeds. And by now I was calmer and I began to sing, "row, row, row your boat merrily down the stream, merrily, merrily life is but a dream."

"Do not sing so loud, girl, it is echoing all around the hills."

"Oh, alright." I pushed the boat up to the grassy bank and jumped out and held it steady for the wizard to get out but he just walked off the boat without the boat moving at all.

"Right, girl, not far now. Pull out the boat as we will need it in a bit." And he began to walk away.

"What do we need the boat for?" I looked for some way to pull it out of the water.

He turned around. *"Do you want to swim to Glastonbury now, girl, as there is one and a half miles to go as yet of water and marsh?"*

"No, I do not want to swim in this uniform again if I can help it, and not in this dark water at all," I replied to him.

"Good, then come along and pull that boat up to the top of this hill, my girl."

"Hey, can you not use some magic to get it up that hill?" I cried.

"No, girl, I shall need all my magic as you call it tonight when we get to the island as we have to go in through the back door so to speak, so come on and no more backchat." And he walked on.

"Huh, it is all right for you," I muttered and I found under the boat a rope, which I suppose was to tie it up at night with. I grasped it and with some effort, I pulled the boat out of the water to see it was a flat bottom so it was an effort to pull it up this bloody hill. After some effort, I got to the top and I sat down exhausted with sweat running down my back. Not nice on a cold February afternoon, the sun may be out but it was still cold.

As the Merlin was going off somewhere, I lay in the boat and worked out what day it was. Ah yes, I was sick on the 1st of February and I worked out how many days since I rode out of Tintagel and I came up with the 13th of February to the startling revelation that I had been in this mad world for almost two months. Good God that was some shock.

"Oh, so you made it up then?" said the Merlin looking down at me.

"I've found a good spot to lie up till it gets dark so up with you if you want to go home and bring the boat as well."

"Hey, could we not go now, please? I would like to go home today."

"No, we will have to go tonight, girl."

"No need to shout at me is there? Alright, tonight will have to do." And I got up and began to drag the boat after him as he had walked off and out of some trees into a big clearing and I saw a wonderful sight – Glastonbury Tor. I stood in shock to see it as I had so longed to be here.

* *
* * * * * * * * * * * * * * * * * *

"Over here, girl, and sit down. We will wait till the moon comes up as its light is the only way to see my way into the realm of the Fay."

"What? But it is hours yet before the moon comes up!" I cried to him.

"Yes, I know but it is the only time I can do the big spell to get into the realm unseen, girl, so I would suggest you get some food in you and some sleep now." And he pulled out of his robe some bags of food and set them out. So I sat and looked at the Tor as I ate my food and wished I could just get this all over and done with. *"I will wake you when the time is right."* And with that, he put his finger to my head and I fell to sleep on the spot. Only to be awakened by him in the darkness and I found myself all wrapped up in my cloak. *"Come on, girl, we have to get to the lake in time so up you get and pull that boat with you and keep behind me so you do not get lost in the dark."* So I picked myself up and I fumbled in the dark for the rope on the boat and began to pull it down this dark hillside hoping I would not fall into any holes or over logs in the way but at the same time, I was so happy to be on my way at last.

He led me down some way till I found myself in a small valley with a spring flowing into a small river, which we followed down to lots of reeds. *"Right you,"* said the Merlin, *"push that boat in till you hit the water and do not make any noise if you can help it. You never know who is about."*

"But can you not magic it though, it would help."

"No girl, my magic will be seen by the high priestess and it cannot happen if you want to go home tonight."

"Do you mean the priestess on the island does not know you are coming at all?" I asked him.

He just smiled at me in the dark. *"No girl, you are my way in to take over them so I can learn all their secrets, my girl."*

"What, you clandestine mystic, you. You have planned this all this time since I landed in this mad world haven't you?"

"No, but it was very fortuitous for me that you did and when I saw that arm ring of the Fay, I knew I could get into the realm unseen, which is why I have helped you for so long these last two months. Now push the boat into the reeds." And he poked me with his staff.

"Oiy," his staff hit me and I felt queer all over, then he said, *"Go."* And I could do nothing to stop myself from pushing the boat as he got in till I was up to the middle of the water then he pulled me in and put the pole into my hands. *"Right, punt, girl."* And I punted the boat out and over this vast area of the lake. *"Over there, girl. We can get into the flow of the river Brue, which will take us all the way."* And as I punted along the moon came up and lit up the Tor, not that I could enjoy the sight as I was still all wet and cold with Merlin's spell on me to do his bidding.

* *
* * * * * * * * * * * * * * * * *

And slowly we drifted along in the flow of the river and as there were no reeds in the way, I just stood at the bow of the boat until he said, *"Right, push to the right, girl."* I just did what I was ordered to do and pushed hard as we had left the flow and into the reed banks I had to push the boat through until we came to the side of a small hill where he leapt out of the boat. *"Come, girl, leave the boat and put down that pole."*

178

I was compelled to do what he said and pulled the boat onto a dry bank, and then looked up at the moon. "*Look at me. We have made good time thanks to you and that arm ring of yours,*" *he said* as he grasped my right arm and pulled back my blazer's cuff to get to the arm ring of the Fay and he tried to pull it off my arm. "*Why won't it come off?*" He pulled me over to him.

"*Bah, Mab's doing. It will not come off so you come with me.*" And he began to pull me up the hill. "*Now, girl, put your head forward.*" And he lifted my right arm up and he thrust me forward as he shouted some words and suddenly, the red rubies all glowed and shot into the air out of my arm ring and up into the air where the three rubies glowed very red and revealed a door which fell apart as the rubies' light went out to leave a long tunnel of blue moonlight.

"*It worked,*" he cried as he ran up the tunnel with me. "*I now release you, girl, and here is your reward.*" And he pulled me to the other side of the tunnel and then threw me to the ground and pulled off all the clothes he had given me, the cloak and the headdress, leaving me just in my uniform with my bag on my back which I had on at that time. "*Goodbye, my girl. It was nice knowing you so off you go, oh I would hold my breath If I was you, hahaha.*" As I got to my feet to say some bad words to him, he held up his staff and shouted some words at me and I was covered in blue light. "*Now you go. What?*" he said as out of the darkness came some people in blue cloaks who ran up to him.

"*No, not now,*" he said as they got to him. "*I got—got to— Ooops. Oh pooh!*"

"What do you mean by ooops?" I said as the ground under my feet disappeared and I plummeted feet first down into darkness.

* *
* * * * * * * * * * * * * * * * *

And I must have screamed as I fell, for I found myself in one of those horrible long tunnels I had fallen down in the first place, so long ago. But this time there was no water to fall into for which I was grateful and I was still glowing moon blue. It lit up this tunnel nicely as I slid down at an alarming rate. It was hard to focus on anything which was about me.

It was a most unusual thing which happened to me; I began to slide upward. How weird, or so it seemed at the time and then there was light at the bottom of this tunnel, a very small speck of blue light which got steadily bigger and bigger and as I was moving at a fast rate, it was hard to make out what was at the bottom of the tunnel until suddenly; I recognised it for what it was as I could see green growth and blue water. "Oh God, not again." I took a deep breath, remembering what the Merlin had shouted and me, 'Hold your breath.' And then I was in a world of green and blue, bubbles all around me and I could not see anything till my feet hit something dark grey as I sank down. I was covered all over in grey clouds of muck. As I had stopped falling now, I waved my arms about to clear this muck to see my surroundings, and as it cleared, I saw that I was in a weed bed of water lily stems all anchored to the bottom and as I looked down at my feet, I could see they were in a foot of dark mud.

"Damn wizards," I muttered to myself as I tried to pull out one of my legs and as I did so, I saw movement in the weeds. I looked up only to see the biggest blue/green carp you could hope to see with a look of shock and surprise on its face to see me in its home.

"Get out of my pond." And the big carp butted me in my chest.

"Right, that does it. This is the second time I have been attacked by underwater things." I gave it a right hook in the mouth whereupon it swam off into the weeds. As I pulled my left leg out of the mud, I looked up to see very beautiful sunlight above me in between the weed on top of the pond as the fish called it. So up I pushed, my arms down, kicking my muddy legs and I rose up to the surface to come up to the feeling of hot sunshine on my wet face and looked up to see blue sky, white clouds, vapour trails and the sound of traffic. "Yes, yes," I cried, "I am home at last." I splashed the water with my hands and kicked my legs in joy as I looked up at the sky.

Then a voice said, "Where have you come from?" behind me.

"What?" I sank back down then I spun around and came back up to see a man in shorts and a T-shirt with sandals on not ten feet away with a woman with a baby in her arms and a big pram sitting on a green seat.

"Oh, hello!" I cried to him as I swam to the side of the pond. "Can you help me out of this pond, please?"

"Do you often swim in your school uniform then, girl?" asked the man as he put his hands under my armpits and bent his knees and pulled me out of the pond. Once on my knees, I pulled out my wet backpack and stood up where I took hold of his hands and did a dance of joy to be home and spun him around, water flying out of my uniform and drenching his T-shirt to the laughter of the woman on the seat.

"Wow, girl, where did you come from as we have been here for some time and you could not hold your breath that long underwater, so tell me how you did it, and in your school clothes as well."

"I only swim in my uniform when necessary," I said. "Please, can you tell me where I am? Is, is this Glastonbury? And I am so glad to be home and it's summertime and no more bloody winter." I said throwing my arms into the air.

"Yes girl," he said. "Look you are in the abbey and you can see the ruins from here." Whereupon I spun around to see lots of ruins.

"Ah yes," I cried. "Please, can you tell me where is the nearest phone box as I have to ring up my mother to tell her I am back home. Oh" – as I pat my wet blazer – "I have got no money on me. Do you have 10p on you please that I can borrow?"

"Yes, but 10p will not get you far but you can use this." And he reached into his shorts and he pulled out a very small and slim object which was all blue and white.

"Here, you can ring up your mother on my mobile phone and if you cannot get through there are two phone boxes outside the abbey, if you want to, girl." And he held it out to me.

"What's a mobile phone?" I asked him as I took this small blue and white thing out of his hand.

"What do I do with it?" I asked him.

He looked at me very puzzled for a moment. "This is a mobile you can go anywhere in the world and ring up anybody you want by pushing some number in and saying hello."

"But I have not seen one of, what did you call it, a mobile. I have heard of something like it on Tomorrow's World on the TV but not for years to come."

"Tomorrow's World," he said, "that has not been on TV for years, girl. Where have you been?" he said as he took it out of my hand, he opened it up and handed it back to me. And as I looked at it in my hand, there was a colourful picture of the man and the woman with the baby in her arms but as I looked close up, I saw to my horror as I read all in white, *02 – UK – 04 Sept 2015, 13:46*. I closed my eyes as I handed it back to him.

"Please, can you tell me what year it is?"

"Pardon me, did you say what year is it."

"Yes," I said looking down at my shoes.

"Why it is 2015, girl, how can you not know?"

"Argh!" I cried and fell to my knees and punched the ground with my fists and screeched in vexation and sobbed and sobbed my eyes out. In my state of despair, I felt myself being picked up and put onto the seat where I was hugged by the woman in an embrace and held tightly in her arms as I was rocked to and fro. I felt as if my world had fallen from under my feet as I cried.

"There, there, girl. It will be all right. Just give my husband the number and he will ring your mother."

I found my voice and croaked out, "You do not understand. My—my mother would be in her eighties by now and the shock would kill her as the last time I saw her was the year 1970 and now he said it was 2015, which is 45 years into my future. How can this be?" And I began to cry again and sobbed.

"Oh rubbish, girl. How can that be, you are only what 14 or 15. Your mother cannot be in her eighties, can she now?"

"Yes, she can be," I said as I jumped up out of her arms, "I must find my way home." And I looked up and shouted at the air, "Merlin, you bloody stupid idiot. You got it wrong, you stupid wizard this is my future. You did it on purpose to me." And then I began to cough as I had swallowed into my lungs the pollution of this timeline. Then I had a brainwave. I had stopped coughing as the woman was patting my back and I turned to her. "Thank you both for being so kind to me but there is only one person, ah no, power, that can help me now." And I undid my wet blazer and in my inside pocket was the bag of fairy dust which Queen Mab had given to me. Now, what did she say? Only put it on to water to summon her and only in need and yes, now is the time of my need. I walked over to the pond to where I had come out as the water lilies had not come back from my passage where I had swum to the side.

Then I looked at the two people who had helped me so much. "Please look away as it could be most fearful to the baby," I said as I pulled out the bag and keeping it in my shadow as I opened the top and in one swift throw, I cast the dust onto the surface of the water to see it froth and bubble and shoot up into a cone of water then down into a green ten-foot wide hole.

"Goodbye, future world!" I cried as I flung my bag on my back and ran and dove into the green to my uncertain future.

Angelina Janny Jones will return in Book 3 in Deep Trouble.